# A PRESENT FOR PARKER

## THE MERRY EVERYTHING SERIES

### JODI PAYNE
### BA TORTUGA

# A PRESENT FOR PARKER

## A Present for Parker
## Jodi Payne and BA Tortuga

*A Present for Parker is an opposites attract, forced proximity, holiday romance between a rodeo cowboy who's ready to retire and a Vermont attorney who thought his only love would be his historic farmhouse.*

Parker Stephens is a cowboy looking for a place to call home. His only family has kicked him to the curb, leaving him with his truck and the clothes on his back. He doesn't even have his dog. So when he shows up at the Vermont home of his friends Skyler and Beckett, he's got no idea what he'll do beyond the holidays. For now, he just needs to visit and breathe.

Heath Wooledge is used to being alone, working on his vintage farmhouse, and eating a frozen pizza or two. Since he's never been invited to his business partner Beckett's house to eat dinner, it stands to reason they're asking him for a favor. Luckily for him, when they ask if he'll let Parker stay at his place because their guest room is a mess, Heath can't believe his good luck. Parker is a sweetheart of a cowboy, and he's never been more attracted to anyone in his life.

The two have immediate chemistry, but will magic of snowy

holiday Vermont make the two of them accept the gift they've been given?

## THE MERRY EVERYTHING SERIES

Window Dressing

Cowboy Protection

Cowboys and Cupcakes

Thawed Out

A Present for Parker

These books in this series are stand-alone stories. Some of them contain MCs from our other books but you can absolutely read these without reading those.

A Present for Parker
Copyright © 2026 by Jodi Payne & BA Tortuga

**Edited** by LC Hinson

**Cover** illustration by AJ Corza
http://www.seeingstatic.com/
Cover content is for illustrative purposes only and any person depicted on the cover is a model.

ISBN: 978-1-963644-19-7

Published by Tygerseye Publishing, LLC
February 2026
Printed in the USA

*As always, to our wives.*

# 1
_____

Parker sat in the McDonald's parking lot, drinking his coffee and eating his breakfast burrito, and trying to wake up.

He was waiting for it to be late enough to call Sky.

He knew it wasn't officially too early for Sky. The amazing son of a bitch was up at six in the morning, but he'd learned that, if he called before seven and Beck answered the phone, Beckett would threaten to kill him, which was awkward.

Especially with the kids.

No one wanted to be threatened with homicide when his godbabies were listening.

So he waited until 7:05, then crumpled up his trash, threw it in the bag, leaned back in his truck seat, and punched Sky's number.

It took Sky two rings to answer. "Hey, Parker, what's wrong?"

"Does there always have to be something wrong?" Something was wrong, but that really wasn't the point. The point was, it didn't always have to mean something was

2 | JODI PAYNE & BA TORTUGA

wrong when he called. Sometimes he could just be calling to say hello.

"Because you never call at seven a.m. if you're not in trouble or in Australia."

"Hey, that time change is super hard!" He peeked at his phone. "It's seven 'o seven now."

"Whatever. What's up?"

"I was wondering..." And he'd been wandering too.

"Huh?"

"I'm in Ticonderoga, and I was wondering how you felt about company for the holidays?"

There was a pregnant pause. "Are you in Fort Ticonderoga or is there another one?"

"Who's in—wait, is that Parker? He's the only one who calls this early." Beck's voice was in the background. He didn't even need to hear Sky's husband sigh, he just knew. "Parker is where? There's no rodeo in Ticonderoga."

"No. He's coming for Christmas. Cool, huh?" Sky was good to him.

"Only if it's cool..." He wasn't a mooch. He was just... on the outs with the whole of his family.

"But it's only—Oh." There was a short, silent pause, and then Beckett went on. "Oh, yes. It'll be Christmas before you know it. So cool."

"I know. You'll be here by suppertime?"

"Closer to lunch. I want to get off the road and rest for a bit, you know? I'll help do whatever. I promise." He just wanted to be somewhere he was loved.

"We'll have sandwiches. I think Charlie wanted ham and cheese." Beckett's voice was suddenly warm. "Hey. Drive safe, Parker."

"I'll call when I get close and see if there's anything y'all need me to pick up from the grocery store." He swallowed hard, trying to keep the emotion out of his voice. "I really do appreciate this, guys."

"You know you're welcome. Looking forward to seeing you. Later, man." Sky hung up and the call disconnected. He could only imagine what the conversation was between Sky and Beck, but regardless, he knew they were the right people to call.

They'd finally had it out, him and Mom.

He wasn't going to get married, he wasn't going to have babies, he wasn't straight, he wasn't a very good bull rider, and he didn't know what he was going to do when he grew up.

But he knew it wasn't 'stay in Oklahoma and raise goats', and he'd said so.

That had been when she told him if he didn't want to stay, he could get the fuck out.

And here he was.

She had his trailer, his stuff, and his dog.

He had his phone, his go bag, his chaps, his bull rope, and some presents for the kids.

And his friends. He had friends. So he'd get there and get a good night's sleep for the first time in a week.

All he had to do was make it there in one piece and breathe.

## 2

Heath stared into his freezer, trying to make a decision.

Pepperoni.

Four cheese.

Very veggie.

Ham and pineapple.

That one had been sitting at the bottom of the stack since he'd bought it, which might have been over a year ago. Did frozen pizzas go bad? Did it matter? He had no plans to eat it anyway.

Oh. Sausage and mushroom. *We have a winner.*

His phone rang as he reached for it and, when he saw who was calling, he almost didn't pick up. It wasn't that he didn't like Beckett, but it was Friday, and he'd left the office early on purpose. Still, he wasn't going to ghost his business partner. Also, Beckett didn't understand that a text was always preferred and would just call back in an hour, so he answered it.

"Hey, man. What's up?"

"Hey, Heath. Do you want to come to dinner tonight?"

He blinked, startled by the random invitation—the random *last-minute* invitation. Spontaneity wasn't really in Beckett's wheelhouse and, on top of that, he'd had dinner at Beckett's house exactly never in all the years they'd been working together. They'd been out to bars, restaurants, both with and without Skyler, but dinner at Beckett's house? Never.

"You there?"

"Oh. Sorry. Uh... dinner tonight? I don't—uh—" *Shit*.

"Why not? You know you're just staring into your freezer anyway."

"I am not!" He closed the freezer very quietly.

Beck started chuckling softly. "Uh-huh. Sky's cooking..."

"Sky cooks?" Huh. He'd had it all wrong. "Is he the one who makes your lunches? I thought you did that."

"Oh, hell no. That's all my husband. I can help, but I just do what I'm told in the kitchen."

He frowned. "Well, what's he making? Is it good?"

Really? Had he simply asked that just like that?

"Enchiladas. Chicken enchiladas with homemade verde sauce. And there's guacamole and chips and salsa. I believe he also bought a tres leches cake for dessert."

Oh, damn. That was way cooler than frozen pizza.

"What time do you want me?"

Beckett laughed. "Maybe six? We'll have some margaritas and then sit down for dinner."

What was happening here? Was Beckett buttering him up for something? Retiring? Dying?

"No one's dying, are they?" Yep. He asked that. Heath rolled his eyes. Go him.

"Heath, would I invite you to celebrate my impending demise over enchiladas?"

There was a bark of laughter in the background, which

could only have been Skyler, and now they both knew he was an idiot.

A book-smart, lawyerly idiot.

"That does seem unlikely. I will see you at six."

"Perfect. Come hungry. Bye now."

The line went dead. Come hungry? He was already hungry, he was about to cook a—no, he wasn't. He sometimes made other things for dinner, right? Like, uh, pasta. And scrambled eggs. He made some seriously mean rye toast.

He looked down at his after-work attire—boxers and a T-shirt—and decided he'd better go find something to wear. Did one dress for enchiladas?

Jeans. Skyler was a cowboy; jeans were always appropriate.

Also, it was about Christmas, so an ugly Christmas sweater was also always appropriate.

What should he bring? They were having margaritas, so wine seemed stupid. Maybe something for Charlie, Noah, and the little one. Huh.

"Oh!" Chocolate. He had a bag of chocolate Santas he'd bought for the office in his briefcase. He knew when he bought them that they would never actually make it to the office, but he'd expected to be sucking them down over an episode of *Shrinking*. It was probably better to give them to the kids.

He looked at his watch. It was after five already, and he needed to get moving. He dashed up the stairs and found jeans, then dug out his ugly sweaters, picked the most kid-appropriate, and pulled it on.

The last-minute invite from a non-last-minute guy was still bothering him. Not bothering in that suspicious way but bothering in the he was dying of curiosity way. Were they already having a party and he was on the B-list? Were they having another baby? Maybe they needed a last-minute babysitter and were bribing him with food.

Which, by the way, would absolutely work.

It didn't matter; he was just intrigued.

And late. He was running late.

He finished brushing his teeth, combed his beard, pulled on his black-frame glasses, which were more casual and fun than his wire-framework glasses, and checked himself out in the mirror.

"You are way too handsome for this sweater." It had a big polar bear on it. It was perfect.

Well, it would be perfect if he had someone for it to be perfect for. He was having a bit of a dry spell, which you know, he could only do so much.

He headed down the stairs, pulled on his winter cap—it was waterproof and lined with cozy fleece—tugged on his coat and gloves, stomped into his boots, and he was out the door.

Damn. He should have remote-started his Silverado to warm it up. It took a minute to get out of the house in the winter.

He was going to be a few minutes late, so he texted Beckett.

HEATH

Just getting in the truck.

He'd get there.

And then he'd find out what was going on.

Sky had put him to bed in the man cave on a recliner the second he walked in the door.

He hadn't even had lunch.

Just, "Here. Bed. You look exhausted. We'll talk when you get up."

It'd been weird but, to be honest, he'd been awake for so long, he just crashed.

He woke up to little Sierra patting his cheeks. "Uncle, wake up! Papa is cooking."

He cracked one eye open. "Papa or Pappy?"

She giggled softly, and he hugged her, tickling her gently. "Papa."

"Good because Pappy should not be cooking."

"Oh, you'll make Pappy cry." She grinned at him. "Papa's making 'chiladas. Chicken ones."

Oh. They were going to be so good. He hadn't eaten real food in days. Truck-stop and fast-food burgers were not Sky's enchiladas. His mouth was already watering. "Best I get up then, huh?" He should help. He needed to help so he felt like he wasn't a mooch.

He pretended to let Sierra haul him out of the recliner, groaning at how stiff he was.

There was laughter from the other room, one of the voices so deep and resonant he knew it couldn't be Sky or Beck. Didn't sound like any cowboy he knew either. Shit, he wasn't company ready. He tucked his shirt in and ran his hand through his hair.

"Who's here, Bug?"

"Heath."

"Do I know Heath?" he asked.

She shrugged. "He works with Pappy."

Oh, so Parker didn't know him. He really wasn't the kind of person Beck introduced to other lawyers.

"So there I was, hip waders up to my chin standing in three feet of water and—" Beck looked up as he and Sierra shuffled into the room. "Hey, look who's up."

"I told him Papa was cooking." Sierra seemed proud of herself.

"Thank you. Come here and give Pappy a kiss, baby girl."

Sierra darted over and leapt into Beck's arms. "Pappy! Pappy, I love you!"

Charlie rolled her eyes with all the drama of a ten-year-old going on forty. "Uncle Parker, hey, we only have one more day of school until Christmas break."

"I bet you're happy. Vacation for the win, right?" He was the cool uncle, he didn't have to be all pro-school, right?

Charlie nodded. "Oh, yes, so happy. So tired of school. I just wanna go out and ride horses. Instead, I have to learn how to do stupid division."

"Division is very useful when you have to split everything by three." Beck gave her a look and, boy, did she give him one right back.

"Three, six, nine, twelve, fifteen, eighteen, twenty-one—"

"Okay, okay." Beck laughed.

She stuck out her tongue. "I want to *divide* my time between hiking out in the mountains and barrel racing. Right, Papa?"

"Yes, my girl. You are my cowgirl, but you have to know your multiplication and division and how to read. It's important." Sky winked at Parker. "Otherwise, how do you run your own event?"

"Fine. Two times two is four, four times four..."

Beck pounced on her and started tickling, and she screeched and giggled.

"Not in the kitchen, buttheads." Sky shooed them out and Beck dragged Charlie toward the couch. It was an open floor plan, so they didn't go far, just out of harm's way. "Heath, this is Parker. Parker is a bull riding buddy. Parker, Heath is Beck's business partner."

"Good to meet you." Heath held up a beer and nodded to him, deep voice filling the room. Heath wasn't all that tall, but he seemed to take up a lot of space—the voice, the solid build and broad shoulders, and a big smile framed with a neatly-trimmed beard.

"Pleased." He nodded over, smiled. Pretty, pretty. "It's really good to meet you. Noah, dude, where are you?"

A little boy came barreling across the room, Legos falling from his lap. "Uncle Parker, you're awake! Dad said not to bother you, and I didn't, so I get a gold star on my chart!"

Charlie rolled her eyes. "On his chart."

"Charlie," Skyler snapped, arching an eyebrow and glaring at her.

To her credit, she backed right down. "Sorry, Papa."

"Deathtraps." Behind her, Beck was already picking up the Legos.

Heath glanced at him, making small talk. "What brings you up to snowy Vermont?"

"I found myself at loose ends for the holiday, and I was missing my best friends, right, Charlie?"

Charlie nodded, grinning over at him. "You needed a soft place to land."

Oh, such a smart, smart girl.

"I did. Thanks for letting me come over."

"We didn't *let* you; you're always invited." Beck wandered back to his beer and picked it up. "Parker is basically family."

"That's cool." Heath glanced at him and then looked at Sky. "Skyler, dinner smells amazing."

"Green chile and cheese are two of the things that make the world go 'round." Skyler nodded to him. "You feel better after your nap?"

"I'm nowhere near as sleepy." Feeling better? Eh.

"Long drive?" Heath asked him. "They can really wear you out."

"Yeah, I came up from Oklahoma, so it was a long day." It had been a damn long day that had started as a damn long night. He didn't want to get into it with a stranger.

Hell, he wasn't sure he really wanted to get into it at all. He just wanted to lick his wounds and be here, surround himself with people who were happy.

Sky gave him a sidelong look but thankfully didn't ask in front of Heath either.

"Well, please. Don't feel like you have to be polite or social on my account. That sounds like quite a trip."

Parker detected no lies, but he intended to find his center here, get his mind in the middle. "It was a trip, but it's over. And I'm here, and I'm happy, and there's going to be enchiladas."

"I know I'm looking forward to them. It's my first time here for dinner. Isn't that funny?" Heath shrugged. "We've been business partners for years, but we always go out."

"That's because we leave the kids home for grownup social engagements." Beck leaned on the counter near Sky. Close without quite being in the way, like two people who love each other get. "It's tough to have people here unless they're ready for family time."

"Good thing for y'all, I'm always ready for family time." Parker loved these babies, and he wanted a family, friends. He missed riding, he missed being with all those cowboys.

"Good thing." Beck gave him a follow-me wave. "Come on, Park, let's set the table."

"You know it." Four adults, three little ones—that was seven plates and seven forks. Bingo.

Beck put out placemats, and he found the plates without having to ask where they were. He'd been here so many times that everything was familiar.

"So... Oklahoma to Vermont is about seventeen hundred miles, give or take. I looked it up. That's more than a day of straight driving, right?"

"Yeah. It was a long one." His shoulders started to creep up around his shoulders. Beck was too smart for his own good.

"You want to talk about it?" Beck was keeping busy, not looking at him, just setting the table and acting like he was just making conversation.

"Mom threw me out. Like all the way. So I'm... here." There wasn't a better way to put it, really. *My mom hates me. Hi.*

That stopped Beck, who looked over at him this time. "Well, fuck. I'm sorry, Park. Sky has told me a little about your mom and... how she is. You came to the right place though. We've got your back."

"Thank you. I didn't want to spend Christmas in my truck. I knew y'all would have room for me here."

"Well, actually, Park, about that." Beck turned and looked at him. "We are down a room right now. There was a leak and we had to fix... some stuff, and Sky is painting... would you be terribly hurt if I asked you to stay with Heath for a little while? He has a house not too far and extra room and—I mean, you can come here any time of course and play with the kids or whatever you want, but we've got pretty tight quarters right now."

His lips actually parted. Oh. Oh God. He hadn't even considered there wouldn't be room for him. "I'll go get a hotel room. No worries."

"Oh. No, no. Sky would never allow that, and you know it. Heath is a good guy; I've known him a long time. Maybe just try it out until we get the room put back together? It won't take too long. We're really sorry; you know this isn't how we want things. You're always welcome here."

"Are you sure he won't be put out? I don't want to impose on a stranger."

"Heath? Oh, as soon as I told him our predicament, he offered right away. He knows you're not a stranger. You're family. You'll like him once you get to know him a little better. You guys will get along great."

"Oh. Well, if he doesn't mind, but I can get a hotel room. Honest." He didn't know what to do, to be truthful.

"He doesn't. We've worked together a long time, and he's happy to do us the favor. No worries. And I promise as soon as Sky is done fixing things up, the room is yours. Okay?"

"All right. If it's all good. Only if." Parker just wanted to be... welcome, dammit.

"Of course it's all good. We're always here for you, Park. You know that." Beck handed him a handful of forks.

"Yeah, but there's a difference between here for me and bothering some guy I don't know." And that was the truth. He didn't want to put anybody out, just wanted to believe he was part of something.

"Yeah, I hear you. I really don't think it's a bother, but I get it. How about you just try it out, and if it doesn't work, then we'll figure out something else. Okay? No stress."

"Okay, no stress. I do want to help with Christmas. I have stuff in the truck for the kids." Quite a bit of it actually. Money wasn't one of his problems.

"You're the best uncle they have." Beck clapped him on the shoulder. "You good finishing up here? I need to check on Heath."

"I can totally set the table without help, and if I need help, Charlie will come." He had no doubt.

Beck snorted. "Knowing Charlie, she would put forks under everybody's seat so that they would jump when they sat down. She's in her naughty nine-ten-eleven whatever however long it's going to last phase."

"Oh, I know that one. I'll let you know when I'm past it."

"It's too late for you." Beck laughed and shook his head as he left the dining room. "Thanks for your help, Park."

He sighed and set the table, humming "Jingle Bells" as he worked.

---

"So, yeah." Heath tossed his beer can in the recycling. "Once this deal closes tomorrow, I'll have a lot more time."

"I'm sure you have something in the pipeline," Beckett said, walking back into the kitchen.

Sky glanced up from the stove. "Hey, everything good with Parker?"

"Everything's good. You mind if I borrow Heath? Park will be done in a minute."

"Nope, he's all yours."

Married couples were so weird. It seemed like there was subtext to everything they said. Like you were always missing an in-joke.

"Come on in the office, Heath? I want to ask you about something."

Work. Of course. Friday night and Beckett wanted to talk about work. So, dinner was a ruse to get him here to work late?

So damn unfair. He was here for company and enchiladas.

They went to the office, and Beckett smiled at him. "So... I have a bit of a problem."

"Sure. Like I said, I'll have some time on my hands after this deal closes tomorrow. Assuming it closes." He flopped into a comfy chair in the corner of the room.

"It's really not about work. It's more personal." Now that was odd. Beckett really wasn't personal.

Oh. Crap.

"Shit, are you okay? I mean—sorry, I don't want to be nosy but, whatever you need, you know I'm here."

"No, no. I'm fine. We had a bit of a leak in the guest room. It's a problem, and Parker just showed up. Usually, wouldn't be an issue because he brings his travel trailer, and we just assumed, when we told him he could come, that his fifth wheel would be here. But it's not.

"He's having family trouble, and he no longer has his trailer, you see. He doesn't have anywhere else to go for

Christmas. So, I was wondering if there was any way on earth you could possibly let him use your guest room.

"He's very polite, very clean. He's got his own truck, so he'll be bringing himself over here a lot. I just need a place for him to sleep."

He blinked at Beckett as everything became oh, so clear, and he wasn't sure how he felt about it. Beckett never asked for anything, and he did have a lot of extra room but... "So, let me get this straight. You invited me to dinner to butter me up so you could ask me to take in a stray friend? No wait, a stray friend of Skyler's. A... cowboy?"

"No. I asked you to supper to eat enchiladas. Parker is willing to sleep in the recliner downstairs or to get a hotel room. We thought he'd be more comfortable with friends."

"Wow, man. I'm not an asshole. I'm not going to make one of your friends sleep in a recliner. Damn." Look at Beckett calling him out. "But...what am I going to do with a cowboy?"

"Give him a cup of coffee and smile at him. Talk to him. He's one hell of a storyteller."

He nodded. "Sad he has nowhere to go for Christmas, huh?"

"More than nowhere to go. His mother threw him out. Took his travel trailer. Everything." Beckett looked a little queasy about it.

"God. That's... I'm so sorry. That's awful." He could only imagine how that felt. His family had always been supportive. "Yeah. He should totally stay with me. It's fine."

"Thank you. Seriously. I just feel so bad for him. He's a good guy." Beckett snorted softly. "You know, I used to hate him. Like absolutely hate him."

He wasn't sure whether that was encouraging or not. "I

guess I'll reserve judgment then. I'm sure it will take him some time to settle."

There was an unholy screeching sound followed by loud cat hissing, and Parker came flying into the room, panting. "Walter found me."

Heath tried not to laugh, he really did, but it was hopeless. "Walter...?"

"Walter. That damn cat..."

A furious howling set up, Walter absolutely homicidal.

Instinctively, and a little absurdly, he grabbed Parker by the arm and pulled the man behind him.

"Walter Thaddeus Alan Jackson!" Skyler's voice was coming from the kitchen, but it silenced the whole house. Everyone froze. "Go to your bed."

"Does that actually work?" he whispered to Beckett.

Beckett shrugged. "Most of the time."

Walter glared but slunk off, tail puffed up like a bottle brush.

Heath blinked back at Parker, finding striking blue eyes under the shock of blond hair. "What did you ever do to him?"

"Nothing. I swear to God, the only thing I ever did was try to feed that son of a bitch."

"What the hell did you feed him?" He snorted a laugh, tried to contain it, then gave into the giggles.

"I remember that." Beckett chuckled.

"Look, I was new at this whole cat thing, and his person, his dad, was all broken, and I had to call Beckett who hated me, and it was just a shitty situation. I didn't do anything to that damn cat except be worried near him."

Beckett elbowed him. "See? I told you I hated him."

"You did tell me that."

"Parker was a big help during Skyler's wreck. I got over

myself." Beckett put a hand on Parker's shoulder. "I think Walter just associates all that worry and stress about his person with you."

"Uh-huh. Either that or he's possessed by a violent demon and wants to steal my soul." Parker shrugged. "Six of one, half dozen of the other."

"Probably just as well you're not staying here, he might scratch your nuts off in your sleep." Heath deadpanned that one, hoping for a laugh. He wasn't good at one-liners, but even he knew a hook when he heard one.

Parker guffawed, the laugh strong and honest, and it was sweet as hell. It felt good, knowing someone thought he was funny.

He got a shake of the head from Beckett, who obviously didn't know a good joke when he heard one. He chuckled though, thinking he and Parker might make it work until Beckett and Skyler got the flood or whatever under control.

"You need another beer, man?" Heath gave Parker a smile.

"Yeah. I'll take one more." Parker was a little like Sky, and he could only remember Sky having more than two beers... once?

Maybe?

"Good. Me too." He wouldn't be having more than two either, he had to drive after all, and these remote Vermont roads were windy.

"Come on, guys, dinner is ready. Walter will be good. Charlie? Get your sister's hands washed please. Noah, use the upstairs bathroom and scrub those fingers."

The kids scattered as the adults gathered in the kitchen. Heath felt like he should be doing something other than standing around. "Can I help?"

"Sure. Grab the squeezy sour cream. The kids will want

it for sure. Oh, and the bottle of ranch. Only Charlie will eat the spicy ranch."

"Ranch and squeezy—ah, got it."

Beckett pointed to the dining room. "Go sit, Park, I'm right behind you."

Heath closed the fridge door in time to catch Beckett giving Skyler a thumbs up and a big grin. Skyler made a celebratory gesture in return with his fist.

Huh. They seemed awfully excited about the enchiladas.

"All clean!" Noah came running in and screeched to a halt about two inches from him. "Sorry, Mr. Heath."

"No worries. Go sit. I'll follow you."

"Okay, did you know that Santa Claus is coming? Santa Claus is coming. He's gonna bring presents, and I'm gonna get a bike."

"You hope you're going to get a bike. You still have some time left to be naughty or nice."

"No. No, Pappy tell him! I asked real good! I write-d a letter." Noah stared at Beckett with huge eyes.

Beckett put a hand on Noah's head and looked at him. "Noah's right in this case. He wrote a kind letter and asked very nicely, and Santa wrote back and said not to worry, he'd get a bike this year."

Oops. "Oh, that's special. That must have been some letter. Santa doesn't always have time to write back." That was a good save, right?

"I worked hard. I spelled *big* words."

Charlie rolled her eyes, but he noticed she didn't argue.

"That's so cool. I know your dads must be proud of you." He set the salad dressing down on the table.

"We so are." Beckett pulled out a chair. "Sit everybody. Let's eat."

"It smells so good, Sky. Thanks, man." Parker smiled and nodded to Sky. "I love when you make enchiladas."

"They're a family favorite for sure."

Beckett waited for Skyler to sit down and then raised his glass. "To family."

Heath followed suit, very ready to drink to that. He caught Parker's eye, since they were going to be roommates for a while. "Hear, hear."

## 4

———

Parker stared out the living room window, listening to Sierra jabber at him about her bath, her baby doll, all sorts of shit.

She was adorable.

Hopefully, Heath was cool with him spending the night. Otherwise, he'd be sleeping in the recliner.

Dammit.

"Sierra-berra, it's bedtime." Sky came in and scooped her up. "Say goodnight to Uncle Parker."

"Night, Uncle Parker."

"Good night, baby girl. Sleep well." He blew her a kiss. "I'll see you tomorrow."

"Night-night. Night-night," she sang as Sky brought her over to Heath.

"Night, Sierra." Heath smiled at her and gave her a little wave.

"Goodnight, pumpkin." Beck kissed her head. "Sleep tight."

Heath stood up. "Hey, man. Thanks for having me. This was fun. Skyler is a really good cook. I'm stuffed."

"He will take that as a compliment." Beck shook Heath's hand. "Park? You good to follow Heath home?"

"Are you sure it's cool, man? I mean, I really do appreciate you letting me crash." And he'd be the best house guest for a night that the man ever had.

"Of course. I live alone, I have a second bedroom, so you're totally welcome." Heath pulled his keys out of his pocket. "You want to drive your own truck, or drive with me?"

"Do you mind if I ride with you?" Two beers was one too many on icy road.

"Nope, I'm good. Why waste the gas? Do you have a bag or...bags?"

"I have a duffel, yeah." He knew how to travel. It had been his whole life.

"Thanks again, Heath." Beck walked them to the door. "We all really appreciate it."

"Sure, sure. Night, Beckett."

"Thanks, man. I'll see y'all in the morning." He'd promised Charlie they could go shopping together.

"Sounds good. Night." Beckett gave a wave and the door closed behind them.

"Grab your bag. I'll start my truck." Heath left him standing on the front stoop.

He took a deep breath and then made his way to his truck, slipping and sliding all the way over. He made it without falling on his ass, thank God for small favors.

It was damn cold out, but Heath's truck was warming up. "You need some winter shoes. Pick some up while you're shopping with Charlie. I turned on your seat heater."

"Yeah. I totally need to." Seat heaters were the coolest thing ever. Pun intended. "It'll be worse tomorrow, huh?"

"Well, it'll be normal. We don't think snow is bad up

here." Heath grinned over. "But if you're not used to snow, then yes. It'll be worse."

"I've seen a bit of snow when I was riding, but usually if it was snowy, I'd fly in, you know?" It was just easier.

"Sure. Well, I'm your ride back tomorrow, so don't stress it." Snow was actually falling lightly as they pulled out of Sky's driveway. "Have you been up here many times?"

"Oh, yeah. I was here when Sierra was born. I am here for Sky's event every year at a minimum, and then if they need pet sitting, I can do that." He didn't want to talk about Walter, dammit.

Heath laughed. "What do you do with Walter when you pet sit? I mean...that animal has it out for you. I've never seen that before."

"I pray. A lot." He looked over and grinned. "Also, he does like his food."

Heath cracked up. "Everyone has their Achilles heel."

"You know it. Some of us have had theirs repaired more than once, even." God, he amused himself.

"Oh. Ow. Really?" Heath glanced at him. "That's a horrible injury."

"Yeah. I've had mine surged on four times. It can be harsh." But it was part and parcel of the whole genie gig.

"Damn. Does it hurt all the time?" The roads had no streetlights and, as the snow got heavier, all he could really see was a tunnel in front of them where the headlights were shining on the road. "Looks like we left at the right time. Should be home in twenty minutes or so. I'm taking it a little easier with the weather."

"No problem. I'm in no hurry." And hurting was just part of life, wasn't it? It didn't help a bit to worry about it.

"Well, I'm sorry you can't stay with Skyler and Beckett.

They're good people. Sounds like you'll be able to get back over there in a few days maybe."

"I really appreciate you letting me crash. I can't tell you how much it means." Parker hated knowing that he was putting someone out.

"I have some idea. Beckett may have mentioned...a little."

"Yeah, what can I say? My mom and I have always had a bit of a rocky relationship, and well, I'm not getting any less gay..." It was weird because he didn't say that word very often. He sure as shit said it now.

"I'm sorry, but you have to be you, right?" Heath shrugged. "My mom is a super-ally. She's the one wearing the Free Mom Hugs T-shirt and rainbow boa at the Pride parade."

"Oh good for her. Seriously." He had never been to a Pride parade. He couldn't imagine him doing that. Or someone like Skyler going to one? They might be gay, but he didn't want to get killed.

He just wanted to be him without having to stress about everything all the time.

"She's a lot, but in a good way. She means well and she loves me, so I won't complain about the enthusiasm." Heath turned down a narrow road, and he could see a light, and then two, and then a house came into view, a warm glow coming from the downstairs windows. "That's my place. Almost there."

Attractive. Nice. "I like it." Whatever it was, it was better than a hotel, and he'd take it.

"Thanks. It's just a little farmhouse in the dark, but wait until you see the view in the morning. Especially off the deck. I didn't buy it for the house, or for the commute, which is longer than I'd like. I bought it for the view."

"I can't wait to see it." He wasn't even being sarcastic. He loved taking pictures of new places, new sights.

Heath smiled over at him, then pulled into the driveway. "I'm lazy about shoveling. Sorry. There's a path if you want to slide over to my side to get out." Heath stopped the car, and sure enough, the passenger side was pretty snowy. He'd probably be up to his knees.

Heath climbed out and stepped back, holding the truck door open. "It's a little slippery too, so be careful in those boots."

"I'll try. If I fall, catch me." He winked. God knew Heath was bigger than him by a goodly amount. Surely the man could make a catch. He looked like he had really nice hands.

"You got it." And Heath looked oddly eager to try too. He slid out of the truck, hit the path and, sure enough, his boots kept on sliding. Heath grabbed him under the arms and knees, picked him up, trudged the maybe ten feet to the cleared off front porch and set him down like he was carrying a child.

"No broken bones on my watch." Heath laughed and went back for his bag, boots making crunching sounds in the snow.

"Thanks. I feel like a newborn foal out there, but it's sure fun." He was going to spring wood if he wasn't careful.

"You looked like one, too. I'm sure I have an extra pair of boots with better traction than those. Beckett probably wants you back without a broken neck." Heath closed up the truck, shouldered his bag, and made his way back, pulling keys out of his pocket. "Boots and anything snowy comes off in the mud room. There are slippers and flip-flops and stuff there if you want shoes. The floor, especially downstairs, can get cold. Come on in."

Those were a lot of words, but he followed enough to hear, "Take off your damn boots," so he did that.

"Cool." The stairs going up were right outside the mudroom and Heath set his bag down there and went to a wood stove in the corner of the cozy living room. There was a deep couch, a recliner, and a huge TV. "You want anything? Beer? Tea? I like a hot tea at night."

"I'll take a tea, sure. Thank you." Beck drank tea, so he'd tried it. It was okay.

"Yeah? Cool." Heath stacked wood in the stove, and it came to life, making that familiar roaring sound before Heath shut the door. "I have lots. Do you want caffeine? If not, I have herbal and decaf. Come on in the kitchen. It'll warm up in here in a minute."

"What do you usually have?" He knew mint for upset stomachs, regular, chamomile for old ladies, and iced.

"Oh, I have this vanilla chamomile that's really nice before bed." Heath snorted. "I can't cook, but I can boil water for tea."

"Rock on. I can grill a steak and a hot dog." He winked over. "And I open a potato chip bag like a master."

"Yeah? You should see me with a frozen pizza. Mwah." Heath made a chef's kiss gesture with his fingers.

"Dude, you speak my language. Frozen pizza is proof we are loved." His favorite ones had the little bitty chunks of pepperoni.

Heath shook his head. "Don't say that out loud around Beckett. He's harsh."

"He doesn't like pizza? I swear, he's a bit of a nutbag." That was unnatural.

"Frozen pizza. He thinks I'm some kind of lonely frozen pizza eating recluse." Heath snorted and set a kettle on the stove. "He's right about the frozen pizza, I guess. Did you want to settle in? I'm sure you're ready to get some sleep. Beckett said you'd been driving for hours. I can bring you tea up when it's ready."

"Whatever works for you. I'm good at socializing. I'm good at going away. I'll take the bag up and then come back for the tea."

"I'm definitely not sending you away. I just don't want you to feel like you have to be polite. I get it. Or, well, I don't really get it, but I understand it's been a tough few days for you."

"Then let's sit together. Chat. I like meeting people."

"Cool." Heath nodded. "That couch is super comfy. Do you like honey or sugar or something in your tea? I like a splash of milk and a little honey."

"Honey, please. I've never had milk in tea, so I'll maybe not do that." He wasn't sure that sounded doable.

Heath laughed and pulled two mugs out of a cabinet. "As you wish. So you rodeo?"

"I do." At least part-time. He was damn tired, and he had cash, so he wasn't covering as many bulls as he used to.

"Do you ever ride in Skyler's event up here? I've been every year. I don't remember you, but I always find it kind of overwhelming." The kettle sang, and Heath filled their mugs.

"I'm always here. It's pretty early in the season, and it's fairly close after finals. If you make it all the way to finals and you don't come out of it hurt, you're not trying hard enough."

God knew he'd been hurt for most of Skyler's events.

"I'm not going to pretend to understand it, but I like to watch." Heath handed him a mug and sat on one end of the couch. The stove was really starting to warm the room up and make it cozy.

He grinned and forced himself not to tease, 'I hear that about you,' and he went with, "It's a complicated sport in some ways. In some ways it's super easy. Stick for eight."

"Yeah, no. That looks impossible to me. It's impressive that anyone can do it." Heath blew on his tea and tried a sip.

"Thanks. It's something you've got to love, I think." Why else would someone do it? It was hard on a body.

"I guess everything is that way. Most people wouldn't put themselves through a zillion years of law school if they didn't want to be a lawyer either. It's good you've found something you love to do."

He nodded, because what else could he do? Seriously? He was going to ask Sky to help him figure out his next move.

After the holidays.

Heath sipped his tea. "Warm enough? The stove usually does a good job down here. I do have the heat on for upstairs though."

"I'm good. This is a neat house. Have you been here a long time?" See him make small talk.

"I bought it like, ten years ago? It was a fixer-upper then. It's in much better shape, but still a bit of a labor of love now. Beckett loves to tease me about it. He used to call me Bob the Builder."

"Oh, yeah? That's cool as hell. That makes it more yours, doesn't it?" He loved that idea, to make a place something special.

Heath gave him a bright smile, even his beard seemed to stretch happily. "It does make it more mine. That's exactly it. I get to look at the back deck and know that I built the damn thing. Or the brick floor the wood stove is sitting on, or the kitchen island. I'm proud of the place."

"No shit? That's cool. I built out Sky and Beck's basement room with our friends." He'd loved doing that.

"Yeah? You guys did a great job. Beckett says the kids love it down there. They really needed a space to stretch out indoors, since the winters get cold around here."

"Yeah, it started as a man cave, and then we added the rec room." Those kids had a whole little world down there.

"This spring, I'm going to build a balcony off my bedroom upstairs. The view is amazing. I want to be able to sit and drink my coffee and watch the mountains light up in the morning and the sunset at night."

"Oh, wow. That's going to be amazing. You don't have neighbors to peek in?"

Heath laughed. "My neighbors are deer, moose, eagles, foxes, the occasional coyote or bear, wild turkeys...oh and sometimes Jake Tigg's dairy cows get loose and wander over."

"I've never seen a moose!" His eyes went wide. "Are they the biggest thing you've ever seen?"

"They can get pretty damn big. I was joking with Skyler once that they are like if you took a bull and stretched its legs about four feet. All top-heavy and bizarre-looking. But they are neat animals. Tall, strong, quiet. They really are majestic."

He tried to imagine Bushwacker with legs like that, and it was enough to make him a little dizzy. Damn, that would be intense as shit.

"Stay long enough, and you'll see one. Or several. If you're lucky you'll see a mom and a baby. If you're really lucky? You'll get to see a bull." Heath was very relaxed and seemed to be enjoying his tea. "Are you a music guy? A TV guy? Movies?"

"I watch a ton of movies, and I love music of all kinds

except opera. Opera I don't get, you know?" He didn't understand all the yodeling, but it was mostly because it was hard to understand.

"Opera is way too foreign for me. I mean, I can't knock their talent, but the whole thing—" Heath made a grandiose gesture and opened his mouth in a huge "O".

He couldn't help his grin. "Right? And the hats with horns and stuff. I just don't understand at all."

Heath chuckled. "Nope. Give me football any day. Any damn day."

"Now you're speaking my language. Who's your team? I'm a Chargers fan, myself." He didn't really care. He just loved watching the guys play.

"Pfft. I'm New England all the way. And while you're up this way, you will be too." Heath grinned at him, the beard making Heath's smile seem bigger.

"Fair enough. I remember when the Patriots used to be good..." he teased.

Heath snorted. "Yeah, man. Me too." The snort turned into a chuckle, and then a big belly laugh.

Okay...that was pretty.

Like genuinely, dearly pretty.

He probably shouldn't stare, should he?

"Damn Patriots." Heath hauled himself off the sofa with a groan, and he got a look at the tight fit in the ass of the man's jeans. "Okay. Let me show you around upstairs. If I'm tired from being up since six, you've got to be toast."

"Sounds good. Thanks again for this. I do appreciate it." He stood and took his cup to the sink, washing it out.

"What time did you want to head back to Beckett's tomorrow?" Heath joined him at the sink, then took his cup from him and set them both in the drying rack. They were shoulder to shoulder for a second and he could smell

Heath's cologne, or maybe it was aftershave, woody and warm.

"Whenever you're ready. I'd take you to breakfast, if you want." It was only fair, he thought.

"Thank you, but there's really nothing between me and Beckett but cows. We can make some eggs here, and you stay warm indoors and watch me shovel us out."

"Fair enough." He could get out there and dig in the morning. He was a tough bastard.

A tough, tired bastard.

"Come on." Heath led him up a narrow staircase to the second floor. He could tell that less work had been done up here; the wood floors were a little warped and creaky and the banister wobbled a bit. But the vintage molding, glass doorknobs, and the wood-frame, double-hung windows were really neat. "I've got two extra rooms up here... I decided this one was probably the most comfortable for a guest room. I use the other as an office. And my room is at the end of the hall there at the back of the house."

"Good deal. Thanks so much. I hope you sleep well and shit."

"I usually do." Heath nodded. "Your bathroom is there, and there are towels in the little closet. The bed is made because my mother actually warned me that random house guests happen. I told her they don't happen to me, so she will be thrilled to learn she is, once again, right." Heath took a few steps toward his own room. "Good night, Parker."

"Good night, sir. Have a good one." He waved and headed to the bedroom. Lord have mercy.

He was going to have to have a long shower, jack off, and crash so he could get up in the morning and shovel.

God help him.

# 5

Heath rolled out of bed and right into his slippers. He loved his house, but the floors were cold on a winter morning. He pulled on his robe and tied it tight, hit the head, then scurried downstairs to pump up the thermostat and stoke the wood stove.

Once things were cooking, he made a pot of coffee and took some eggs out of the fridge. He hoped his house guest didn't mind plain old eggs; he didn't really know how to do anything fancy. He had some cheese...

Fortunately, Parker seemed pretty low-maintenance because he really wasn't set up for house guests. He lived alone, did his own thing. If Parker wasn't around today, he would have slept in a little longer, skipped breakfast, put on some music, and maybe started refinishing the banisters or something. He had a long indoor to-do list for the winter.

There was no sign of Parker yet, so he decided to get dressed and clean the snow off his truck before he made eggs. He'd debated what he should do first—build the upstairs deck or turn the old barn into a garage. He'd decided on the deck for the spring, but man, now that it was snowing again, it was tempting to change his mind. The snow looked pretty high out the back; his deck had about a foot on it. And winter was just getting started.

He glanced out his bedroom window, shocked as hell to see someone out there—a cowboy shoveling his drive.

Or trying to.

Parker slipped and slid about every third step but, somehow, he managed to use the shovel to balance himself, the man laughing happily.

It looked like a losing battle, but at least Parker was having fun. Why was he shoveling the driveway though? Jake was usually down here with the plow at first light. A foot was a lot, but it wasn't enough to stop a man with a plow.

He started to reach for his phone, and that's when he saw it. One of the big evergreen trees that lined the road had come down right across his driveway.

Damn.

And that was when his phone rang.

"Hey, Jake," he answered with a sigh.

"Hey, neighbor. You got a tree down."

"Yeah, I see it."

"You need a hand?"

"I think I've got it. Can I call you when I get it cleared?" He had a chainsaw. He had two, in fact.

"Of course. And I can send Tim down if you need a hand."

Jake's son was about the size of a twig. "I will do that. Thanks, Jake." He hung up and got dressed so he could go rescue the L.A. cowboy from the snow.

The guy was going to freeze to death, and then he'd have to explain that to Skyler and Beckett.

Worse, the kids seemed to like him too.

He tugged on his boots and gloves and grabbed another shovel. "Okay, cowboy, I'm coming." He trudged out into the snow. "Hey, Parker? What are you doing out here? Are you warm enough?"

"Hey! You said you needed shoveling done, so I thought I'd help!" The man's lips were blue. Literally.

Whoa. Damn. Time to get Parker back inside.

"You rock. I really appreciate it, and you're doing a great job. Can I make you some breakfast? Why don't you come on in and have some coffee, and we'll eat something before we get back to it?" They could discuss not shoveling and breaking down that tree instead once Parker wasn't...blue.

"S-sounds fab. This shovel is great for steering. I approve." Parker winked at him, obviously playful and happy. It was adorable. It made Parker even more handsome.

"Steer yourself back to the house, then. I'm right behind you." In case the guy fell. He didn't though. There was a lot of sliding and laughing, but they made it back to the house in one piece. "You're pretty wet, and that's going to be uncomfortable. You'd better take those jeans off. Socks too."

He didn't need to see Parker without his jeans on. That smile already had him warmed up in ways the fire didn't, so he left the mudroom, calling over his shoulder. "Do you have a robe or...dry sweats or something?"

"I do. You got a dryer I can borrow, by any chance?" Parker worked his boots off and left them in the mudroom.

"Yep. Laundry is in the basement. Help yourself. You want me to run upstairs and get something for you?" He should really be a good host and go put Parker's things in the wash. He sighed and went back into the mudroom.

He heard the schlump of denim hitting the ground.

"I can just toss this shit in, and then I'll run up. Where's the basement door?"

"I'll put it in for you. The basement is chilly." He held a hand out for the wet clothing, trying not to peek like a stupid teenager when they were both grown adults. "You just run up and change."

"Are you sure? Thanks, man. I'll be right back down." Parker hurried off, and he got sight of a man covered in scars and tattoos, not an ounce of softness anywhere.

Damn.

He watched Parker all the way to the stairs and stood there a second even after the cowboy was out of sight. He'd never seen anything like that.

He snapped out of it and got Parker's things in the dryer, then came back up and got busy making eggs and trying to think of anything other than all that muscle and the stories on Parker's skin.

And that tight, tiny ass in navy blue boxer briefs.

Jesus.

It just screamed, 'touch me'.

And he was not going to. Not. At all. He was going to scramble the living fuck out of these eggs and try not to burn the toast and not think about Skyler's friend *that* way.

Although, Skyler obviously wasn't thinking about Parker that way.

Skyler stared at Beckett like the man was stunning.

He shook his head and pushed the toast down in the toaster. The only cheese he had was American, so he broke that up and stirred it into the eggs, making sure it melted. He got out butter and strawberry jelly. He set out two mugs for coffee.

Watch him play host. He could do this.

Parker came bouncing down, grinning at him. The man's energy was wild. "I can't stop shivering!"

Heath glanced up at Parker, who still looked kind of frozen. "Go sit by the wood stove." He ducked into the mudroom and came back with a down vest that Parker was going to swim in, but it would help keep some heat in. "Pull that on, and I'll get you some coffee."

He put together a plate for Parker, complete with relatively unburned toast and a travel mug full of coffee, which would stay warm longer than an open mug.

"Looks great, man. Thanks."

Was this son of a bitch the Energizer bunny or what?

Maybe he was on drugs.

Either way, if Parker had frostbite once thawed out, Beckett was going to kill him.

"You're welcome." Maybe he should ask Beckett what was up. He pulled out his phone and texted.

HEATH

> Tree fell and can't get out. Parker is stuck unless you can come pick him up.
> Does he...

He deleted that last bit and tried a more tactful way.

HEATH

> He's got a lot of energy huh?

He hit send and went to get his breakfast.

SKYLER

> He's fine. The kids are puking. Keep him there. Also, he's a bull rider. They only come in adrenaline-ridden

"So, Beckett says the kids have a stomach thing, and you should stay here." He sat with Parker and picked up his fork.

"Oh my God! Let me call Sky. If I have to, I'll DoorDash them some soup and salt crackers."

That was cute and well-meaning but, no. "Parker, I'm sure they'd appreciate that, but there's actually no DoorDash delivery out this way."

"Oh. Well, I'm sure they can... I'm sure if they need me, I'll figure it out. If not, I'll help you." Parker ate his eggs with gusto. That was nice, he guessed.

So, Parker wanted to be needed. He heard that loud and clear, and he figured he could give Parker the perfect job to use up some of that energy. "Random question. Do you know how to use a chainsaw?"

"I have used one a couple of times, and I didn't die." Parker's grin was wicked.

"Cool. Not dying is my only rule." Heath grinned. "There's a big-ass tree down at the top of the drive. If we can get that cleared, Jake can come plow us out. I don't shovel the driveway as a rule. The front porch, yes. The deck? Sometimes."

"Oh. No problem. I will totally destroy the big-assed tree with you."

"Fantastic. I have plenty of gear—boots and gloves and stuff." He wasn't going to let Parker slide around in wet cowboy boots with a chainsaw in his hands. "And after we can come back in, get a hot shower, and make pasta. Or stuff pizzas in the oven and put on a movie."

"Sounds perfect." Parker chugged his coffee. "What's your favorite movie, man?"

"Anything with explosions." He grinned. "Or car chases." He honestly didn't have a favorite. "I like Samuel Jackson movies a lot too."

"Oh, yeah. I will watch anything that's not torture horror. That shit creeps me out."

"I live alone in the middle of nowhere with woods on one side and an open field on the other." Heath laughed. "I do not watch scary shit. Disney is okay though."

"Right? I'm on the road a lot. Like in that scary dude on the highway way."

"Nope. Uh-uh." He chuckled and sipped his coffee. "Sorry you don't get to see the kids today. But we'll get you out tomorrow, I promise."

"It's okay. I'm thinking about finding an Airbnb, stay around a little while." Okay, that was a surprise.

"That's an idea, but, I mean, I've never seen Beckett and Skyler allow friends and family to stay anywhere but with them. Well, except for this little hiccup, but this is only for a few days." The room just needed paint or whatever; it wasn't going to be too long.

"Yeah." Parker didn't sound too sure, but he didn't elaborate, just finishing up his breakfast. "Thank you for breakfast. I appreciate it."

"You're welcome." It wasn't fancy, but Parker didn't seem to care. "Let's find you some boots and then we'll fire up the chainsaws."

## 6

Parker had learned a couple of things in the last few hours—chainsaws jostled a man's innards, trees against the snow were fucking fascinating to look at, this place was fucking cold but beautiful, and it was really easy to underestimate how much he could do.

Heath kept looking at him like he was some sort of strange and unusual creature.

He knew how to work.

He also knew how to party and how to sleep, and he was going to do that sleeping thing here in a bit after he warmed up and got still for even half a second, which was why he was kind of wandering.

Because one, he was fucking freezing, and two, it seemed rude to just fall asleep when there was a pizza in the oven.

"So where are you from? You said you were a Chargers fan so... L.A.?" Heath was watching him again; this time it seemed like with more curiosity.

"Oklahoma." Parker shrugged. "I've been all over the country, really, traveling, but I was born and raised in Oklahoma."

He'd never had the slightest desire to build himself a home there in Oklahoma. He liked the coasts and the mountains, but he just wasn't into the prairies.

"I know exactly nothing about Oklahoma except there's a song named after it." Heath frowned. "Haven't warmed up yet, huh?"

He shook his head and smiled. "It's flat. That's really all anyone needs to know."

"Okay, then I now know *Oh-klahoma*." Heath sang the last word as he pulled the pizza out of the oven. "I shouldn't sing."

Parker cracked up, but he didn't think it was all that bad. He'd heard Mackey bellowing Christmas carols like a bull moose in rut.

"Listen, if you're cold, I have a closet full of sweaters. Go grab one. Maybe one of the fleece ones? And I have wool socks, top right drawer."

"You don't mind? That would be amazing." And he'd be...less panicky idiot, teeth chattering, shivering goofball.

At Heath's nod, he jogged upstairs to grab the sweater and socks. His feet were blocks of ice.

He found a sweater and tugged it on. It was big, but soft and warm. Then he went to the bureau and tugged the drawers open.

On the right side were socks, on the left, was...oh dear.

He closed that right up.

Nope.

No no no.

No sex toys.

That was...a little more personal than he needed to be with Heath.

"Pizza is ready! Did you find everything okay?" Heath called up the stairs.

"Yep. Just putting on the socks." Oh, Jesus fucking Christ. He snagged the socks and pulled them on.

"Good, good."

His phone rang in his pocket, the tone familiar.

"Hey, Beck."

"Hey, Parker. Just checking in on you. Everything going okay?"

"Fine. I used a chainsaw. How are the kids? How are y'all?" Poor Beck. Puking was the worst.

"A chainsaw? Heath is putting you to work, huh?"

"Papa no tickle!" He heard Sierra's laughter over the phone.

"We're fine. Uh...much better. What a day. Oh, boy." Weird. Beck sounded like he'd swallowed a goose.

"At least the baby sounds like she feels better, right?" That was good. She was just little.

"The whole family could have the plague, and Sierra would be bouncing around as usual. Heath is treating you okay?"

"He's sweet as all get out. Seriously. He's been super kind about all this." And he was hot, even if he was off-limits.

"I knew you'd like him. He's a good guy. We've worked together a long time. He loves that house too."

"He's done a shitton of work. He should be proud." Parker could smell the pizza. "Pizza's ready. Do you need anything from me?"

"Pizza." Beck chuckled softly. "No, no. Just checking in. We missed you today. See you soon."

"You too. Tell Sky to wash, wash, wash." He chuckled, because he knew Sky would get it. The last time the stomach flu had roared through the riders, that was Sky's entire load of advice.

"Will do! He's said that about two hundred times already. Bye, now." Beckett was chuckling as the call disconnected.

"Parker? You good? Pizza is getting cold." Heath called from downstairs.

"Great. Beck called to check on me, make sure I wasn't driving you crazy."

"Ha! Hardly. You saved my ass today, man. You were a demon with that chainsaw. I don't know how I'd have done it all during daylight without you. Thank you so much."

"You're more than welcome. You'll be able to use the wood in your fireplace, right?" Parker went to help in the kitchen. "What can I do?"

"You can grab us beers in the fridge. I have a dining table, but it's got my balcony plans laid out on it, and I never eat there. I thought I'd just bring this out to the coffee table with a couple of plates; is that okay?" Heath cut the pizza with a wheel.

"Perfect. I assume you don't have a pet that would steal it." Walter would steal his just to aggravate him.

"No. I always think I should get one, but I don't. I'm not sure I'm mature enough to care for anything but myself. I don't even have house plants."

"No?" He'd had his baby girl pup, but he'd been waiting to get a ton of plants until he settled down.

"Well, that may be more about the almost constant sawdust and construction noise. Plants like calm and quiet."

"They don't mind being on the road..." At least aloes didn't.

"I'll remember that next time I take a trip in an RV. Which is likely to be never since I don't own one." Heath served him two slices, then picked up one of the beers. "Do you like being on the road?"

"Sometimes, yeah." Sometimes it was an adventure. Sometimes it was lonely as fuck.

"And other times?" Heath's blue eyes seemed to look right into him. "Not as much?"

"Yeah. I mean, it's a lonely time, when you get right down to it, you know? I spend four or five days a week with the radio and my phone for company." And he was whining.

"I don't think I could do it. I live alone, sure, but I see people at work every day, and I try to keep busy when I'm home. All that driving alone?" Heath shook his head. "I guess you have to really love riding."

He guessed so. "Yeah. It's a real thing."

But what did a man do when he got done? When he was eighteen, it didn't matter.

When he was twenty-one? Still didn't matter.

At twenty-eight, it had started to matter some.

Now it was a thing.

"I'm going to have to find some video on you. I've watched a bunch of Skyler's rides, and it's wild to see him on the back of a bull."

He chuckled softly. "I swear to God, I think Sky was possibly the best rider who's ever lived. He rode like it was nothing at all."

It had been magic to watch.

"He did make it look easy. He had a lot of confidence. He still does, actually, just not on the back of a bull anymore."

"Right? Now he spends all that on wrangling babies and other cowboys." Parker respected the hell out of Sky.

"Imagine if he and Beckett hadn't worked their shit out? Man. What a loss that would have been. Beckett was not a happy person." Heath took a big bite of a slice of pizza, half of it disappearing into his mouth.

"No. He hated me back then. I mean, hardcore hated

me." It had sucked for Sky. He didn't really know Beck all that much, but it had hurt Sky.

"You'd never know that now. The way he talked about you when you needed a place to stay? He cares about you a lot now. I think he was in a bad place then. He spent a lot of time alone; I think he drank a little too often. You know, not happy type things."

Parker nodded. He did know. "He thought I was sleeping with Sky. I wasn't. I wouldn't, and more important, Sky would never, but he thought so."

"Oh, wow. Well he kept that to himself. I had no idea." Heath reached for another slice. "Anyway, they're ridiculously happy now. I'm a little jealous." Heath winked at him and took a bite of the pizza.

"I'm a lot jealous." He dug in, finding the pizza actually delicious—crispy and spicy with a good amount of cheese. He approved.

"I'll get you over there tomorrow. I can hear Jake out there with his plow now so all I need to do is clear off the truck, and we'll be good to go. I've got a garage in the plans, but that might not happen until next year. I'm only one me, you know?" Heath tossed him the remote.

"I get that. If I'm here in the spring, I'm happy to help." He was seriously thinking about only riding a couple of events. He didn't have but two sponsors left, and they were happy with him.

"If you're here, I'll take you up on that. But you'll be off riding by then, I'm sure." Heath set his plate down, rolling his left shoulder. "Man, I overdid it on my shoulder. It's kind of sore."

"Oh man. You want me to work on it?"

"I don't...do you mind? I feel like I pinched something, you know? Like right...here. Ow." Heath snorted.

"Sure. No problem at all." He had been rubbing shoulders for years. It was a problem they all had, at one time or another.

"Cool." Heath shifted on the couch so he could reach more easily, and sighed the second his hands landed on those tight shoulders.

He used his thumbs, digging in as soon as he found a bunch of screaming muscles, rolling the broad shoulders good and hard.

"Oh, fuck." Heath's head dropped forward. "That's exactly the spot, oh my God." Heath's low moan was a little strained. "Damn."

"Deep breaths. In and out. That'll help a bunch." He knew this.

"Okay..." Heath took a deep breath, ribs spreading and stretching Heath's well-worn Green Mountain Boys T-shirt, then blew it out loudly. "Breathing. You have really strong hands."

"You know it. I have to hold myself on a spinning bull." It made for a bit of grip.

"How did you learn to ride?" Heath took another deep breath and let it out. He could feel those tight muscles starting to relax.

"I grew up around rodeo, did junior bull riding before I got my card." He'd been born into it.

"That's cool. My dad was a lawyer. Not quite the same thing, but I get growing up around something." Heath groaned and stretched his neck. "If you ever wanted a second career, I would seriously consider masseur."

"You have to go to school for that." He wasn't that smart.

"Could be worth it." Heath chuckled. "Your hands are—" Heath stopped talking abruptly.

"You okay? Did I hurt you?"

"No, uh. Nope. I was going to say...well, I almost made things weird." Heath chuckled a little nervously and got up off the couch. "Sorry. You want another beer?"

"Sure?" Had he done something wrong? He shifted away from Heath, giving the man some room.

"Cool." Heath started cleaning up their plates. "How was the pizza?"

"Good? I mean, really yummy." He stood, a little unnerved. "Did I do something wrong?"

"What? No. No, I'm just an idiot. That felt great. I feel way better." Heath rolled his shoulders, then headed for the kitchen. "See? All good. Thank you."

"You're welcome." He nodded, totally uncentered and not sure what he was supposed to do.

Heath puttered around the kitchen, cleaning up, then came back with two more beers. "Here you go. You should just feel free to help yourself, you know?"

"Thank you, sir." He nodded and smiled.

God, he wanted to go...home.

Even more than that, he wanted a home to go to.

## 7

W hat Heath had almost said last night was, "Your hands are better than sex." He'd almost said that, and what's worse is that it might even be true, since he couldn't remember the last time he'd had sex.

God, he couldn't remember the last time he had sex.

He sort of remembered the last time he got off with another man, but he wouldn't call that sex, it was more like desperate rubbing off fueled by alcohol and hope, but he never saw the guy again. He didn't even remember the guy's name.

Heath understood he was destined to be alone, and he'd accepted that intellectually. He poured his thoughts and his energy into his house and into work, both things he actually loved to do. But apparently his dick wasn't on the same page, because Parker's strong, warm hands had made his shoulders relax and his balls ache.

That would not do at all. That was wildly inappropriate. This was a close friend of Skyler's who was stranded and had nowhere to go for Christmas. This was not a man to be getting ideas about, or to be fooled around with. Parker was a house guest, and that was all. A house guest who was very off-limits.

Plus Parker clearly had zero interest in him and would be on his way as soon as he was ready to ride again.

They'd watched a movie and then gone their separate ways to bed, and things felt weird this morning as they drove toward Beckett and Skyler's place. Or maybe he was just feeling weird—Parker seemed to be... Parker.

"Feel free to find something on the radio." He turned off his road and onto the wider, but still quiet, county road.

"What do you listen to normally? I bet you're an NPR man."

He laughed. Was he that transparent? "Guilty as charged. *All Things Considered* is a staple on my commute. But I also like rock and country and a little pop."

"Beck's an NPR guy too. I figured y'all had stuff in common."

"We've known each other a long time. He's an excellent business partner. We make a good team." The plow had been through here and the sun was bright today, so the road was nice and clear. "Do you ski?"

"I have. I suck at it, but it's so much fun." Parker turned to face him. "I've done cowboy days at Steamboat a bunch, and I even went to Gay Ski Week in Aspen once. *Fancy.*"

"Gay Ski Week is a thing? I love it." He pictured a whole mountain covered in rainbows. "I haven't seen anything that fancy here, but everyone is equal with skis on."

"It's a big deal out there—parties and all sorts of things. It's wild." Parker snorted softly. "Wild and way too fancy for this old boy."

"Sounds too fancy for me, and I know I'm older than you are." Parker looked about twenty. Well, his face did, the cowboy's eyes seemed older.

"You think? I bet I'm older than you'd guess."

He glanced over at Parker, then back at the road. "I was just thinking that you look about twenty but your eyes...they hold more. If you're asking me to guess? Twenty-five. Tops."

"Aren't you a sweetheart? I'm thirty-one, or will be in February."

He laughed. "Oh wow. I was just a little off, huh? And I'll be thirty-two...in February."

"Oh? What day?" Parker beamed at him.

He rolled his eyes. "Valentine's Day."

"Ha! Mine is the fifteenth. You know how much discounted heart-shaped candy was at my birthday parties?"

"Yeah, everything leftover from the full-priced shit I got at mine." He grinned and shook his head.

"Well, I love it. You're a year and a day older than me. That's not hardly a thing." Parker was laughing, so happy.

Parker loved to laugh. That was the one thing he'd learned about the cowboy in the last twenty-four hours. And laughter looked good on Parker too. Heath snorted and smoothed out his beard. "You still look like you don't need to shave, baby face."

Parker sighed, the sound dramatic as hell. "True that. I am not real fuzzy. I do like that in a man, though."

*No flirting with Skyler's buddy.*

He'd already made things awkward once, so he just played it cool. Or tried to. "Well, you're in the right place. Beards are popular up here. Lumberjack-chic." That was good. Not flirty, not pointing out that he had a beard or that adorable, baby-faced Parker was pretty much exactly his type.

Once upon a time, when he had a type.

"Good to know. Yours is hot as hell. Suits you to the bone."

"Yeah? You like it?" That was absolutely the wrong question to ask, and yet...

Go him.

*Goddammit.*

"God yes. I think it suits you to the bone, and it looks soft. Gives you a jawline sharp as a razor and fits your mouth like—" Parker swallowed and pinked. "It's good."

He fixed his eyes on the road and pretended he hadn't happened to glance over at the exact moment that man blushed. Timing was everything, and it was so pretty on Parker.

He'd pretend he hadn't noticed that too.

"Well, thank you. You uh—you sound like a guy that appreciates facial hair." Stupid. That was the stupidest thing he'd ever said in his whole damn life.

He liked the compliment though; he was proud of his beard and considered it more than looks. It was part of his personality.

"Maybe it's envy, maybe it's just sheer lust, who knows?" Parker's chuckle was soft, self-deprecating. "Do you have family you're going to see for Christmas?"

Just sheer lust. No big deal.

Unless you were crushing on the guy who just told you that.

He really hoped this house guest thing was short-lived. Parker was killing him.

"I do. I'll go to my mom's. My sister and brother and their families will all be there too. She actually has a condo in the same complex as Beckett's parents. She moved there after Dad died two years ago, when the house was just too big for her to deal with."

Parker offered him a nod. "That's a nice complex. I

helped Beck's folks unload their moving truck. It sounds like a great time."

"It's a lot of company, for sure. I love it for a day. I get my niece and nephews all sugared up, and then I go home." He laughed. Really though, they were all getting a little old for that. Last year it was a lot of ear buds and texting.

"There you go. How many do you have?"

"I have one niece and four nephews. My older sister has twin boys; they're sixteen. My younger brother has three—the boys are twelve and ten, and my niece is seven. He has his hands full for sure." He loved all those kids. "We're a crowd when we all get together."

"It sounds like it. I'm going to take Charlie out today, if she's feeling better. If not, we still have a couple of days."

"Cool. I won't stay long. I'll get right out of your hair. I have a wobbly banister calling me." And he needed to breathe some air that Parker wasn't also breathing. Break this spell, or whatever it was.

"Well, if you need some help... I'm handy as a pocket in a shirt, or so I'm told."

"You are. I don't think I know anyone I'd have asked to handle a chainsaw, but you were a pro." Parker had handled it like it weighed nothing, which for someone his own size he understood but Parker was much smaller.

"It was fun. My muscles were all jittery and my hands were numb, but I'd do it again in a second."

"Yeah, I don't need to do that again any time soon." He grinned. "That shoulder thing was real, man. And imagine how I'd have felt if I'd had to do it alone? And how long it would have taken me?"

"We're not meant to have to do things like that in solitary. We're social animals."

He shrugged, then glanced over at Parker. "You think? Weren't we just talking about all the time we spend alone?"

"We were, but it wasn't a joyous talk, and at the end, I was able to see the cowboys."

"True. Well, we can be joyous chainsaw buddies." He turned onto Beckett's road, which was bumpy and narrow and so Vermont.

"Yes, sir. Sounds like a deal." Parker offered him a tentative smile. "Hopefully my truck made it through all the snow."

"It might be snowed in or buried, but it'll be there. I'll help you dig it out, no sweat." He pointed up the road at a house with a pitched roof, a red brick chimney and dark shutters. "Their house is so pretty after new snow, isn't it?"

"Yes. They have a great home." There was a deep pain in Parker's voice, a loss.

He reached out and rested a hand on Parker's thigh. "You'll find yours. You'll find it, or you'll make it on your own terms. Just wait, you'll see."

Parker met his eyes, so serious. "Maybe. Maybe I'll just be the friend who couch surfs around. Everybody needs one, right?"

Heath parked next to Parker's snow-covered truck, then returned that look. "Some of us have a whole room to offer, and you're welcome to it."

"Thanks. I—Thank you." Parker held out one solid calloused hand.

He lifted the hand he'd left resting on the cowboy's thigh and shook. He hoped his smile was reassuring. "You're welcome. And be warned, there are kids in snow suits coming for you."

A snowball hit the passenger side window.

Parker's eyes lit up. "Want to come and play?"

"You're not dressed for this weather..."

"So? I won't freeze. How often do you get to play in Christmas snow?" Parker winked at him. "Come on, we can take them!"

Then Parker opened the truck door and bounced out of the cab, roaring at the top of his lungs.

They had Christmas snow every year, but to be fair, it had been a long time since he'd played in it. He jumped out of the truck, following Parker's lead.

The cowboy was definitely going to freeze.

Somebody had to look after him.

## 8

"Hey, man, you having a good time with Heath?"

Parker looked at Sky and shrugged. "Yeah, I mean, I don't think he likes me very much, but he's been very sweet. He's been very polite and hasn't fussed at me or anything, but you can tell. He's not even into me. He don't care for me even in a friendly way." He raised his hands up and let them drop. "It sucks because I think he's cute, but he's been very nice letting me stay, and it's a great little room. Now that I have my truck, I can stay there one more night and then try to find another place, or I can always crash in the recliner if I have to. He's got plans for Christmas and everything."

And he was babbling—partially because he was cold, and partially because he had horned in on his best friend's Christmas. And really, he thought he was just gonna get in his truck and go.

There had to be somewhere, somewhere isolated that he wouldn't be messing with someone else's holiday.

Or maybe he'd go to a big city and then there'd be tons of people whose holiday was alone, and he could just be another person in a sea of people. Maybe that was what he should do.

Boston maybe?

Hell, if he left pretty soon, he could be in L.A. Wouldn't take but a couple days. He could see stuff and just go to L.A. and pretend like he was a movie star.

"Parker. Heath likes everybody. We sprung this on him is all, and he's kind of a loner. He's probably just not used to house guests." Sky put a mug of coffee in front of him. "You think he's cute, huh? Yeah, I caught that."

"You don't think he's cute? He's neat and good-sized, and his beard is hot, but man, you should have seen it. He'd hurt his shoulder, and I rubbed it, and he freaked out on me. I don't even know if he's gay..." Not that just because somebody was gay, they had to think he was hot, because that was creepy, but he would like for the guy he thought was cute to think he was hot, because who wouldn't?

"He's very gay." Sky leaned on the counter. "Does he know you're into him?"

"Well, I told him I thought his beard was hot. He told me that there are lots of men here with beards, and I should look for them." So he was going to go with yeah, Heath knew.

Sky rolled his eyes. "So, let me just... I want to recap something for you, Park." Sky held up fingers as he talked. "So you gave him a back rub that made him uncomfortable. You told him his beard was hot, and he deflected like anyone in Vermont could have a hot beard. And he hasn't said or done anything that would make you think he was interested? Nothing at all?"

Parker was pretty sure he was really confused. "I don't think so. I don't know, Sky. I think maybe I shouldn't have come..."

"Don't say that." Sky moved around to his side of the kitchen counter. "We're glad you're here. You came to the right place. You're family."

"I want to be." He looked at Sky. "It hurt me. She threw me out like I didn't mean nothing. Like I haven't paid the bills on that place for the last fifteen plus years. She just tossed me out on my ass. Kept my trailer. Hell, she kept my dog."

Sky sighed and shook his head. "Parker, I—"

"Wait. Who kept your dog? Your mom?" Heath came in, deep voice making him jump. "I mean, I don't know why she gets to keep your trailer, but your dog? She doesn't—that's—no."

He looked up into those pretty dark eyes. "Right? I mean, she's a good dog, and Momma won't hurt her, but I've had her for a long time."

Heath frowned. "Well." Heath shrugged. "We have to go get her."

"What?" He nodded, though, because it wasn't right, was it? Stealing a man's dog. It was worse than wrong, it was mean.

"Yeah. After Christmas. We close the firm between Christmas and New Year's, so...let's go get your dog. And maybe even your trailer too. You're going to need it, right?"

"It'll be something to live in while I'm figuring myself out, for sure."

Sky gave him a sympathetic smile. "You finally retiring, man?"

"I'm never going to win anything, and I got me two sponsors, bud." So yeah.

"Hey. God knows I could use someone who knows the business to help with my event, so don't sweat the spring. Coffee, Heath?"

"Sure. Thank you. Retiring, huh? Sounds tough."

"We can call it quitting, but that sounds less classy."

"Less classy maybe but way more empowering. Retiring is saying I can't do this anymore. Quitting is more like, I don't want to do this anymore. Take this job and shove it, man. I'm done." Heath winked at him, then picked up his coffee and sipped it.

Parker took a deep breath and blew it out. "You know what, you're right. I think... I think I'm done."

There. He'd said it out loud.

He was going to puke.

Sky put a hand on his shoulder. "That's a big decision, Park. But I like the idea that you get to quit on your terms. I might even be a little jealous."

"Yeah. You did it the absolutely wrong way, man." He smiled at Sky, because he'd been scared as fuck for his best friend.

"The worst. I am such an idiot." Sky laughed and put an arm around his shoulders. "Okay. Nothing but fun until Christmas."

"And then a road trip." Heath glanced at him. "Hey, what's your dog's name?"

"Sheila. She's a Teacup Yorkie." And the best travel dog on earth.

Heath shook his head, clearly suppressing a laugh. "Not...at all what I imagined."

"I know. She's...she's fierce. She isn't scared of anything." Not even bulls.

"Huh. Does she get along with your mom?"

He shrugged and sighed but told the truth. "She does. She's a good, loving dog."

Even evil mothers could be good to dogs.

"She's still yours."

"Kids are out." Beck appeared from upstairs. "Except Charlie, she's got her headphones on."

"Your girl is growing up, Sky," he teased. "Pretty soon the boys—"

"Nope. Don't. I will beat your ass, man."

Heath laughed so hard he snorted.

Beck pulled a beer out of the fridge. "Seriously. Don't. We're terrified."

"Of the boys or Charlie?"

At his words, Heath lost it, just howling.

Beck shot Parker the bird. "I will let Walter out of the basement. And you." Beck mock-glared at Heath.

"Yes?" Heath was still laughing, his voice high-pitched.

"If you wake Sierra up, you're going to go sing to her until she falls asleep again."

"Well, shit." Heath's laughter turned to quieter giggles.

"Lord have mercy." He laughed harder than he had since he didn't know when, and it felt good to share it with these three guys. It felt damn good.

Sky went to the fridge and traded everyone's coffee for beers. "I'd say we've reached beer o'clock."

They each took their beers, and the day had gone fast with playing and running around. Now the sun was down. Damn.

He'd always heard things moved faster as a guy got older; was this what they meant?

"How are those fingers, Parker? Thawed out?" Beck looked him over. "I hope you bought some things for yourself while you were shopping with Charlie—gloves, boots."

"Yes, Dad. I even let Charlie pick them out." The entire getup was bright blue because she said it made him stand out in the snow, so she could find him when she needed him.

"Charlie said he was going to be an easy target in a snowball fight." Heath punched him in the shoulder. "Sucker."

"Absolutely." For these kids, he'd be a total fool.

"A sucker with dry feet anyway. You're the best uncle ever, Parker." Sky held up his beer. "To Uncle Parker."

"Hey! To Uncle Parker!" Beck held his up as well.

"To Uncle Parker." Heath smiled at him, dark eyes twinkling happily.

"To the babies who make me Uncle Parker." He nodded and drank deep.

## 9

"That was a good day, huh?" Heath reached over and turned the radio down a little. "I haven't thrown snowballs in forever. I'm a terrible shot." Parker had been quiet most of the way home, and he figured somebody had to break the ice here, they were almost back to his place.

"Thanks for the ride, man. I'm sorry about my truck. I think I just need a new battery." Parker rolled his eyes and sighed. "Sky swears it's just the sudden cold."

"He's probably right. I'll give you a jump tomorrow, and we'll get you fixed up. It's not like we weren't both going to the same place." He pulled into his driveway and parked a little closer to the front door than usual. Parker had boots now, and a coat, but it was really cold out there.

"Yeah, and I probably had one beer more than snowy road driving would allow."

"See? You have a designated driver and everything." Heath pulled his collar up and found his house keys before getting out of the warm truck. "Jesus. It's bitter tonight, huh?" He hurried to the house and wrestled a little with the frozen lock before the door opened.

Parker was right next to him, little body too close, too right for comfort.

Heath opened the door, then put an arm around Parker's shoulders, ushering him into the house. He hadn't thought to leave any lights on and naturally the first thing his house guest did was trip over the boots in the mudroom. "Whoa." Heath took one long stride and caught Parker around the waist, setting him back on his feet with little effort. "Wow. You're light as a feather." Solid, but light.

"Gotta be to ride like I do. Did. You know. I ride with balance."

He stared at Parker, arm still around the guy's waist, thinking that if he knew Parker just a little better, he could make a joke. A little innuendo. But he didn't, and he shouldn't, and why hadn't he let go yet?

"I watched some video with Skyler while you were out shopping with Charlie. You looked amazing to me."

"Yeah? Thank you." Parker stared up into his eyes. Literally stared into him, and it made his mouth dry.

"You look pretty good right now too." An icy breeze blew in the still-open door making him shiver. It was like a sign or something, telling him to cool down. "Oh. Damn." He let Parker go and turned to close the door.

"That's a bitter wind, isn't it? What can I do to help with the fire?"

He thought they'd had a moment there, but Parker seemed less interested now. He should have known better than to throw compliments around; he was just making a fool out of himself. "You want to stir up the coals in the stove and see what's still burning? Then we can put some wood on it and stoke it up." The heat would go right up the stairwell and warm up the bedrooms.

He needed to turn some lights on too, so no one tripped again.

"Cool. I like snuggling, but it's no fun with all these coats and such."

He froze for a second and shot Parker a look, then chuckled softly and rubbed the back of his neck, a hundred percent sure he was blushing. "Yeah. Agreed. You want some wine? Or tea?"

"I... I'd like tea please. I don't need to be no more tipsy."

Tipsy Parker was adorable. "Tea it is. You good to get that fire going?" Might as well give the cowboy a chance to figure it out.

"No problem. I've made a thousand campfires."

"Right. I'm sure you have. You like fires? I have a bonfire out back every summer for the office folks and their families. It's a fun night." He put the kettle on because it felt fancier than warming up water in the microwave.

"Oh, I love that. Seriously. I love to camp, to be outside with friends and a fire and a guitar."

"Do you play?" He watched Parker stoke the coals up and add logs to the wood stove like an expert. The cowboy was pretty damn handy despite that heavy sense of uselessness Parker carried around with him. Sure, Parker was giving up bull riding. But he had so much more going for him.

"I do. I'm not fancy or nothing, but I can carry a tune in a bucket. I like making things—whether it's boxes or music."

"Where is your guitar?" He was interested now. "I want to hear you play."

"Oh." Parker shot him a bright, pleased grin. "It's in my truck. Maybe we'll have a Christmas carol sing-along."

He decided on mint tea and poured two mugs after the

kettle whistled. "Perfect. I sound like a moose in rut when I sing, but I'm not shy." He laughed. He wasn't quite that bad.

"Me either. I'm not a great singer, but I do like to do it." Parker winked at him and came right up to him. "The tea smells good."

He held a mug by the top, handle toward Parker. "Right? I can sure boil water." That warm, woody scent wasn't the fire or the tea, it was cowboy. This time, he held Parker's gaze steadily. "I'm having a little internal tug of war over whether you're fair game or off-limits, and neither side has waved a white flag yet."

"I'm open, well over twenty-one, and queer as a three-dollar bill." Parker stepped up into his space, offered him a smile. "And I'm interested. Does that help?"

Yeah, that helped, and the warmth he was feeling wasn't the fire in the wood stove. "Mhm." He leaned a little closer. "Just one little detail—Skyler isn't going to kick my ass, is he?"

Parker set his tea aside. "Why would he? He's way into Beckett."

"Because you're his bestie, and you have a lot going on emotionally, and it's Christmas." He set his mug down too, trying to stay in the moment this time. "And I'm kind of an idiot. A really good lawyer, and an idiot."

"Hush. I want to kiss you. You gonna be cool with that?"

He wanted that kiss so hard he was tingling, and there was no way he was ruining this moment by opening his mouth. Instead, he nodded and bent his head down so Parker could reach him.

Parker reached up, hand sliding around the back of his neck as he brought their mouths together. There was no hesitation in the kiss, no worry.

Just pure, honest hunger.

Parker's confidence was sexy as hell, and he could be honest too. He curled an arm around Parker's shoulders and stepped closer, enough that he could feel the cowboy's chest fill with each breath.

Parker hummed into him, eyes wide open, watching him every second.

He hadn't completely forgotten how this worked after all, and the little hint of tea on Parker's breath made him grin. He slid the tip of his tongue along Parker's lower lip.

Parker purred softly, the sound absolutely luscious, and it didn't surprise him at all when the cowboy opened up for him.

Heath took advantage and found Parker's tongue, sliding them together with a deep-voiced moan. Parker wasn't pushing or rushing, but he could tell there was something a little different about the cowboy. Parker tasted a little wild.

It felt like he was going to have to hold on tight, and when Parker muscled closer, it proved him right.

There was no daylight between them now, and he couldn't get a breath without feeling Parker against him. "Who needs a fire with you around?"

"Mmhmm... I could climb you like a jungle gym. You're so damn solid."

He was that, and Parker was a wisp by comparison. He chuckled low. "Go for it."

Parker's hands landed on his shoulders, and he launched up into his arms, legs wrapped around his waist.

He caught the cowboy, one hand around his back and the other very happily under his ass. "I had a feeling you'd be a handful." He looked up at Parker, who seemed to weigh almost nothing.

"Mmhmm. I'm little, but I can go for hours and hours."

"It's been a minute, but I'm pretty sure I'm good for a

long night." He turned and took a step and Parker's back hit the refrigerator.

"I love how you think." Parker grunted and those legs tightened, squeezing him.

"Not sure I'd call this thinking." Not with the head on his shoulders anyway. Everything else seemed to be pretty with the program. He leaned up and kissed Parker again, sucking on that tea-tinged tongue.

Parker bucked against him, his entire body rocking and riding him, making his eyes cross. His jeans were too tight now, his belly hard as a board.

He spun them again, setting Parker's butt on the kitchen counter so he could use his hands to tug and tear at the man's jeans, wrestling them open. He slipped his hand in and rubbed Parker's hot cock through his briefs.

"Oh, fuck yes. You too. We'll get the edge off, make each other happy as all get out." Parker yanked his shirt up and off.

"Yeah. 'K." He nodded and lowered his fly, popped the button on his khakis, and let them slip low on his hips. His cock went from aching to rock hard as soon as it had enough room, making him moan.

"Mmm..." Parker grabbed their cocks together in his hand, pumping once.

He grunted with it and rocked up on his toes reflexively. "Damn." He pulled Parker into another hungry kiss.

"Uh-huh." Parker's lips parted, tongue warring with his, driving him insane.

The kiss was wild and needy. It was loud too, filling the kitchen with their rough breaths and moans. He added his hand to the mix, curling his fingers around Parker's.

Parker nodded and grunted, his grip squeezing, his lips parted on a deep cry.

He humped into their hands, craving friction, wanting more. "Fuck, so hot."

"Uh-huh. Don't fucking stop. Please."

No stopping, he felt too damn good and it had been too damn long. Parker was his whole universe right now, and his hand around Parker's was giving him everything. He gasped as his balls drew up suddenly. "Park—Parker. I'm—" He groaned, feeling the sound vibrating in his chest. *So close.*

Parker dragged his thumbnail through his slit, pushing just hard enough. "Come on, stud. Gimme."

He hardly had a choice.

"Ah—fuck!" He braced his free hand on Parker's shoulder and shot so hard it stole his breath. The room went dark for a second.

Parker whimpered softly, then more heat spread between them, like Heath's orgasm had drawn Parker's.

They went still together, just breathing. He loosened his grip and tangled their slick fingers together instead, which was way hotter than he thought it should be.

"Damn, stud. You blew my fucking mind."

"You're pretty damn inspiring." He took a quick, light kiss, just for the connection.

"Thanks for...not freaking. I've been thinking about you all day."

"I've been trying not to think about you since yesterday." Heath had to smile. "I freaked out then; guess I got it out of my system."

"Well... I'd like to get you in my...system." Parker laughed, the sound merry and warm.

"We could move the snuggle to my place—room. To my room." Even now Parker still had him a little tongue-tied.

"I'd love that." Parker kissed him again, dragging this one out. "Very much."

He left Parker sitting on the counter and washed his hands in the kitchen sink, then came back and lifted Parker off the counter and set him on his feet. "I'm a big guy. I have a big shower."

"I'm a little guy. I will *totally* fit with you."

"Much sexier than tea." He tugged Parker's jeans up a little.

"Mm...thank you. Let's go be naked. I am so interested in exploring." There wasn't a bit shy about that man.

He put a hand on Parker's ass and steered him toward the stairs. "Go on up. I'm right behind you, taking in the view."

## 10

Parker made sure to wiggle, all the way up to the bathroom.

He was as tickled as a pig in shit to be able to play with Heath. The man was a pure-D stud.

Heath was laughing as they crossed through his bedroom. Downstairs was neat and organized, but the bedroom was full of laundry baskets and the very large bed wasn't made. Everything looked clean, but the man clearly didn't use his dresser.

"It's a bit of a minefield…sorry. I swear I'm a very clean slob."

"Hush. I'm only neat because I live out of a bag." He didn't have anything to make messy. He slept in his truck a lot, and he didn't like the smell of used fast-food containers.

"Hushing." Heath tugged on his pants, and they slipped down over his hips again. "Mm. I'll start the shower."

He got himself naked, then he headed into the bathroom, where the light was low and warm.

Heath started the shower—which took up one whole end of the bathroom—then began to strip. He was built for

Vermont weather, with a good amount of fuzzy hair on his chest to match the beard on his chin, he was broad shouldered, and his muscled thighs were solid like logs.

It was hard to believe the man was a lawyer and not a lumberjack.

"Mm-mm...you are so damn fine."

"I've never thought of myself that way. Strong, smart, capable...not fine." Heath held out a hand to pull him into the shower.

Parker shook his head. He didn't believe that. "You are... a wet dream in my eyes."

He snuggled right in, his cock tucking against Heath's thigh.

"You're definitely making me feel hot." Heath turned his hips so they lined up, then bent and kissed him, one arm reaching past him to close the shower door.

The water poured down on them, and he leaned up into the spray, a soft hum escaping him.

Heath's fingers slid over his shoulder and slowed, exploring one of his deeper scars. "Ouch," Heath whispered the word against his lips.

"Mmhmm...it's an old one." He had hundreds of scars from dozens of surgeries, probably thousands of stitches.

"Scars are sexy." Heath gave him a little push and the shower rained down on his head, soaking his hair.

"Then hopefully you'll think I'm the hottest thing since sliced bread." He went up on tiptoe and stretched, his back popping.

"I thought so before I saw them. Now you're like supernova hot." Heath ran his hands up his sides, then started lathering up his hair. Those fingers found the smaller scars on his scalp, the big one from where they'd wired his neck together, the one from where they took his spleen after a bad wreck.

Heath explored those curiously too, not asking questions but not asking permission either. Heath found a few more as he rinsed the soap out. Heath spent the next few minutes tracing the scars on his chest, his arms, his hips. "So many."

"Yeah. It's a young man's game." And he wasn't that anymore. He was...at the end of this road.

"Are you calling me old?" Heath chuckled, scrubbing him down with a bright pink bath puff. "It was on sale."

"Nope. I'm calling me..." He blinked, then he grinned. "Oh, I get it. Nope. Not at all."

"Ha!" Heath laughed, the sound echoing in the glass-walled shower and circled his balls with the pink thing. "We're not old. We're well-seasoned. Broken in."

Oh, that tingled everywhere. "B-broken in? I can accept that."

Heath winked and traded places, soaking his own hair under the shower and reaching for the shampoo. Heath put on a little show lathering up, letting the soapy suds slip over his shoulders, over the fuzzy chest and across respectably tight abs.

Parker watched, but not for long. He wanted to touch. He'd never been with a man built so well, and it made him a little weak in the knees.

He reached out, starting at Heath's collarbones and letting his fingers drag all the way down, making little patterns in the soap suds.

"You have a light touch for someone with hands like yours, calloused and rough."

He grinned, because it was true. He rode with balance,

and he was known to have a good touch with beasts and men both. "Thank you."

"Oh, thank *you*." Heath took one of his hands and kissed his fingers, then ducked under the spray again to rinse the soap off.

"Mmm..." He made sure every bit of soap was gone from those lovely curls. He was careful, but he did tug a bit.

"Ooh. Naughty." Heath leaned into it, then kissed him again with curiosity, almost like it was a question.

Him? More wicked than naughty, he thought. Still, he opened up, dragging their tongues together.

There was no hurry to the kiss, no agenda, no means to an end. It was just a simple, if deep, kiss and Heath seemed to enjoy it. Enjoy him. When they broke away, Heath shut the water off and grinned at him.

"Nothing about that kiss says Teacup Yorkie."

"No? Have you ever met a Teacup Yorkie in person?" His was a petty tyrant.

"I haven't but I'm looking forward to it." Heath stepped out of the shower and handed him a rainbow towel. "How does she like snow?"

"She's good with it. She's potty trained, and she's a go-baby." Parker sighed softly. And she wasn't his anymore. He had to stop obsessing.

"Good. I was serious about going to get her, you know. I still am." Heath dried off with the colorful towel, then wrapped it around his waist.

"Really?" Sky would do it, if he could with his kids and animals and general busy-ness.

"Yes, really. I'm sure it was chaotic when you left, but now you have a plan, sort of, and I'm sure you don't want to leave her there."

He shook his head. No, he hadn't wanted to leave, but...it

had to happen, he guessed. "No. I mean, Momma wouldn't hurt her, but... I love her. She's my little one."

"We'll get her." Heath took his hand. "It's gonna be chilly in the bedroom. Dive under the comforter, and I'll turn on my little electric radiator. Ready?" He got a grin and then Heath opened the bathroom door.

Parker's balls tried to draw up into his belly, and he scrambled to the bed and snuggled in, shivering into his bones. "Damn Sam!"

"I know, right? I should have cranked the heat up before we went to Beckett and Skyler's." Heath was wandering the bedroom in a towel, moving the plug-in radiator closer to his side of the bed, and not looking that cold at all. "This thing is great though; toasts the bedroom right up."

"Come in, you. We'll share body heat." He lifted the comforter, sucking in a deep breath at the chill.

"Right on." Heath climbed in next to him, skin chilly to the touch at first but they warmed up quickly. "Oh, much better."

"Mmhmm." He wrapped around Heath and held on. God, this felt like heaven.

"That's the first time I've had sex—or anything sexy—in the kitchen."

"Oh? That means we've christened it." Parker approved, all the way.

"We did." Heath combed fingers through his hair. There was something sweet and affectionate about it.

He caught himself pushing into the touch, humming deep in his chest.

He should probably stop that, but he just couldn't.

"You're tired. You've had dark rings under these eyes since the day I met you." Heath slid a thumb under one eye.

"Have I? I guess I've been...dragging my ass."

"No, not dragging. You're totally present. You gave those kids all the attention they wanted today. You helped out. You've been totally in it with me. I'm just worried you're running on fumes and sooner or later you're going to just... stop."

"No. That's not in my makeup." At least he didn't think so. He hoped not.

Heath kissed his forehead. "Okay, good. So maybe you just need a good night's sleep. Or three."

"Maybe." Last night had been the first one he'd had in... forever. He was hoping tonight's was ever better.

"Maybe." Heath chuckled. "What's tomorrow's plan? Back to Beckett's place?"

He wanted to hang with Heath. That was selfish, but true. "I can be real flexible..."

"Oh." Heath's beard stretched with his leering grin. "In that case we better stay home so you can show me."

"Mmhmm... We can play out of the snow." He snuggled right in, hand sliding over Heath's belly.

"Probably good for you to not be frozen for a day or so. Mm. Seriously. Your hands."

"Uh-huh." He groaned, licking a soft line along Heath's collarbone. Damn, he loved that flavor.

Heath tangled their legs together and lifted his chin giving Parker more skin to taste.

Looked like he wasn't the only one who liked it.

"Here I was being all gentlemanly and offering to let you get some sleep." Heath tucked a hand across his nape.

"Mmhmm. I love a gentlemanly man." God, he cracked himself up. He pressed back against the touch, letting the resistance ease his tension.

Heath snorted. "Hell, that guy took a powder." Heath

planted one foot on the bed and suddenly he was on his back with the man hovering over him.

"Oh, hello nurse." That was the hottest thing he'd ever seen, and he was right back in the saddle with Heath.

"Aw, you need a nurse now? Where does it hurt? Maybe here?" Heath went after his nipple and sucked it in between hungry lips.

Jesus, where had this gorgeous motherfucker been hiding his whole life?

He nodded, not even sure what he was agreeing to.

Heath kissed over his ribs and down over his belly. "Don't worry, this won't hurt a bit."

"Mmm...promise? I do love a firm touch."

"Firm, hm? Well, you tell me just how you like it. I'm good for it." Heath caught his prick, humming. "Heavy."

He pushed up, stealing a hard, hungry kiss. "You can have every inch."

"I'm going to give you every inch too." Heath kissed him back and it took his breath away.

If he was lucky, he'd be walking bowlegged in the morning.

## 11

Heath's phone was buzzing. Yes, it was Monday, but it was Christmas week and, like half the office, he was taking the day off. He'd check in later, maybe catch up on some work tonight. Right now he was warm under the covers with an arm around Parker and he had no interest in talking to anyone.

But his phone was buzzing.

Again.

He sighed and rolled over, sliding it off the nightstand and squinting at it.

Beckett.

Shit, okay. He and Skyler were probably wondering where Parker was. He cleared his throat before he answered, but he still sounded like someone had been fucking his throat all night.

Because maybe someone had been.

"Hey. Good morning."

"Morning?" Beckett snorted. "It's one o'clock."

So what? "Is it?"

"Did I wake you up?"

"You woke them up?" Skyler asked in the background, sounding amused.

"Uh." The best lies held a little bit of truth. "Yeah, but no big deal. We were up most of the night watching Christmas comedies." It could have been true. It actually had been the plan for a minute, before the plan had become kitchen sex.

"Mmhmm. Well, the little leak is a bigger leak, so—"

Oh. Darn.

"Well, that's just terrible." A horrible shame. Rats. "I'm sure Parker will be disappointed. But we were thinking—uh, we thought we'd hang out here today anyway. Parker's still not quite thawed out from yesterday."

"Oh? Poor guy. Well, you take good care of him. I know he needs a friend."

Maybe that wasn't exactly what Parker needed...

"Will do. Are you able to get the truck looked at for him?"

"No problem. We'll take care of it."

"Tell Parker we said hey!" Skyler was laughing at God knew what.

"You bet. Will do. We'll check in...uh, tomorrow morning?" He couldn't promise anything today; they had plans to have no plans.

"Good. Great. Have a...nice day." Beckett snorted and was laughing as he hung up the phone.

Were they high? Not with kids in the house, surely.

Maybe one of the kids was being cute as hell.

Warm hands slid across his chest and down his belly.

He put his phone down and rolled back over. "That was Beckett. I told him we weren't going to be there today." He spoke quietly, just above a whisper.

"Mmm...good deal. Poor frozen cowboy," Parker chuckled softly.

That made him grin. "You heard that, huh?"

"It's a great idea—to stay warm and happy." One hand curled around his balls, which were a little sore this morning. They'd been well used last night.

Heath tried not to groan, but he didn't really succeed.

"I was informed that it's one o'clock. So we're right on schedule for not caring what time it is and doing whatever we want."

"Perfect. We were up late, yeah?" Those fingers dragged over his thighs, back to his balls.

"Up late, up early, up in between..." He didn't even bother to stifle the little hiss that escaped him this time. Parker had the most amazing touch, he somehow knew what was just enough without being too much.

"I like when you're up..." Parker's grin stretched against his shoulder.

"You have that effect on me." Probably not for a little while yet though. "I have a confession. I haven't been with anyone in a really long time. You have been pretty amazing."

"No? I think you're hot as fuck. I don't see how anyone could not jump your bones. You're..." Parker squeezed in on him with his elbow, the hug blessedly not echoed in the hand around his nuts.

He didn't ask Parker to finish that thought, he was pretty sure he understood. Instead, he slid an arm under Parker and hugged the cowboy back. "It's nice, not being snowed in by myself. Are you hungry? We could try to not screw up pancakes." He had some frozen sausages too.

"We totally could. I mean, they don't have to be pretty, just cooked through."

Someone sounded like he knew what he was talking about.

"Yep, and I have this great buttermilk pancake mix. You just add water." He tapped his temple. "Smart, right?"

"Brilliant. I love this idea." Parker grinned at him, eyes lit up and happy.

He kissed the cowboy, lazy and slow. It felt good that he could make Parker happy. God knew the man was miserable just a couple of days ago. He started to climb out of the covers and quickly covered up again. The stove was out, he'd bet. He didn't usually stay in bed this long.

"Okay, poor frozen cowboy, it's cold out there. You stay here a minute and let me get the fire going and turn up the heat."

"Do you not need help?" Such a brave man, peeking out of the covers.

"Fuck, yeah. With the pancakes. But let me warm things up—outside the covers—first." He dove out of bed and into his red and black flannel PJs. They were matching top and bottom and he looked like a lumberjack in them but they were warm. He pulled his robe on too for good measure and wiggled his toes into his slippers.

"God, that's adorable. I could eat you up." Parker's eyes were dancing for him.

"You may laugh, but you will not be as warm as I am." He smoothed his hands over the lapels of his robe like it was a tuxedo.

It didn't take him long to get the stove pumping again. He started the coffee first so it was ready by the time he was done. He also turned the thermostat up a few degrees warmer than he would normally for himself before heading back upstairs with two coffee mugs.

Parker had created a little nest, his teeth chattering. "I got my clothes on, but *damn*."

He laughed out loud. He couldn't help it. "Oh my God.

You're either going to die in this weather or you'll grow balls of steel. The jury is out. Here. Coffee." He held out a mug.

"Thank you, and I've been bashing my balls against a bull for years. They're as hard as they're going to get."

He couldn't stop giggling. He ditched his robe and sat next to Parker in bed, not feeling the least bit chilly anymore. "You'll warm up in a minute. I can lend you a sweater too."

"Can you? You're a sweetheart." Parker's cold hand slipped under his flannel and stroked his belly.

"Ho, chilly fingers, man. Drink your coffee." He leaned over and gave Parker a quick kiss. "So. Plans. Breakfast. Then Christmas movies, cocoa, popcorn…a little snuggle on the couch? I hate to be that guy, but I'm going to have to do a little work later too. It's Monday. Technically."

"Oh yeah? I can do stuff, if you need it." Parker grinned. "I can read you your emails…"

"Oh, that'll be a big help. They'll put you right to sleep."

"Do you like it? Lawyering?" Parker drank deep, humming over the coffee.

"I love it." He shrugged. He just did. "I do estate law, so I help people with wills and things. I've done adoptions too. And some other random things." He sometimes did pro bono work for legal services in Burlington, and that could mean just about anything.

"That's cool. That's like feel-good work, adoptions."

"It is. It's the best work. My favorite. It's not enough billable hours by itself, but it's a heavy focus for me. I helped Skyler and Beckett with Noah and Charlie. Terrible circumstances, but good work."

"Oh God. I remember that, and then the little one came early…" Parker shook his head. "But it all worked out in the end, right?"

"They're all happy. That's seems like a win to me." He nibbled Parker's shoulder. "Warming up?"

"I am. You're amazing that way." Parker leaned into him. "My lawyer-jack."

Heath rolled his eyes, grinning. "Great. That's something I'll never live down. You want to get some breakfast? It'll be warmer down there near the woodstove."

"I do, and absolutely. I totally want to." Parker handed off his coffee, which he set on the nightstand. Then the cowboy pushed up into his arms, and eased him up off the bed.

Parker pulled on the sweatshirt while he hurried and found a sweatshirt and another pair of warm wool socks. "That sweatshirt is just a little bit big on you."

Just a little. Parker looked like he was in college.

Except for the morning stubble.

"Yep, but it's cozy and comfy." Parker winked at him as he wiggled his ass.

"Put your socks on," he said with a laugh and leaned in close. "Use the head, and I'll see you downstairs." He gave Parker another kiss and picked up their coffees to take downstairs.

He couldn't stop smiling. Seriously, his cheeks hurt from grinning.

Beckett wasn't going to let him live this one down. Not after all the shit he'd given Beckett about living with a cowboy. It was all in fun, but he already knew it was coming back to bite him.

Parker was going to be very bad for business, but Heath thought it might be worth it.

## 12
_____

Parker didn't mind when Heath was on his computer. He did a little moving around of his money, he ordered a few more Christmas presents, and he messaged with Sky.

SKY

Whatcha doing

PARKER

Watching Heath work. U?

SKY

Same. Charlie's trying to convince the dog to wear a Santa hat

PARKER

Wow. Cool?

SKY

So. How are things? Heath taking good care of you?

PARKER

Yeah. We sorta got it on. Like for real

And he couldn't quite believe it.

SKY

You and Heath? That's great! I mean—was it great? I hope it was great

He sent a thumbs up emoji, then he grinned.

PARKER

Blew my damn mind, swear to God.

SKY

I can't wait to tell Beck. Heath's a good guy.

PARKER

Think he's worried B will be pissed

Which would be a damn shame.

SKY

B is not pissed. Promise. Far from it

PARKER

Cool. Like him

He grinned at the phone.

PARKER

A LOT. Stupid?

SKY

Nope. H is solid. He's anchored here though, just know that

Shit, like he was anchored at all.

PARKER

I got nowhere to be

SKY

Good. Be here. There. We're happy for you

Those three dots danced for a while and then Sky added,

SKY

I want to hear everything

PARKER

Perv.

He would talk, though. How could he not? Sky was his buddy and his soul-brother.

SKY

Uh-huh. Sure. You didn't have to tell me about H but you did.

PARKER

I did.

He wanted it to be real. That was how it worked, right?

PARKER

Babies all better?

SKY

Yes. Climbing the walls. Christmas break is a killer.

PARKER

Bummer. Next year you have 2 in school. Wow.

He remembered when Noah was just barely motivating.

SKY

Not complaining. These kids are just READY for SANTA

Sky added a string of Santa faces and exclamation points which definitely got his point across.

SKY

You coming to us for Christmas or going to Heath's?

Like he'd go horn in on a new family. Beside he hadn't been asked.

PARKER

Yours. Don't want to be weird.

It seemed...impolite at best.

SKY

K. No worries if you change your mind

"Hey, Beckett. This agreement looks okay to me but—" Heath was on his cell phone, obviously talking to Beck. Which was weird since he was texting Sky. "Yeah, that's what I was going to suggest. Tomorrow works. Are you going to be at the office? Oh sure that sounds great. I'll bring the beer. Okay, see you then. Later."

Oh, he liked that—beer at the office. He grinned at Heath as soon as he hung up the phone. "So, where are we having beer?"

"Beckett's place. Tomorrow. They're going to grill."

SKY

Beck says he and Heath have some work to do and you're coming for a BBQ tomorrow

PARKER

Grilling in the snow is WEIRD man

Still, that sounded amazing. "Should we bring anything?"

SKY

Right? Apparently this is a normal Yankee thing. Beck just tromps out on the deck in his boots

"Just the beer. Why, did you want to whip up a side dish? I have zero groceries, and I don't cook, but if you're better at it than I am we can go shopping."

PARKER

Cool. We just bringing beer?

SKY

Yeah man bring beer

"Beer's cool with me." He didn't cook. He bought food that was precooked for his convenience.

Man, Heath sounded grumpy. Maybe he needed a blowjob. It was impossible to be in a shit mood while being sucked off.

"Okay. I am so done." Heath closed his laptop with a definitive swipe of one hand. "Speaking of beer, want one?"

SKY

Ooh. Beck just sighed like the ceiling was caving in. I better go. See you tomorrow

PARKER

cu tomorrow

He put his phone down. "Sure. I'll grab a couple for us."

"Yeah? Thank you." Heath set his laptop on the coffee table and moved to the couch where he'd been sitting. "I wonder if your truck will be fixed. Beckett said they were having someone take a look at it."

"I bet I need to replace the battery. I'm fairly handy." He sat and handed Heath the bottle, trying not to feel the band of tension that the thought of leaving tried to put around his heart. He didn't want to go yet. This was hot and fun and... well, the best thing he'd felt in a month of Sundays. "You ready for me to get out of your hair, honey?"

Heath glanced up, blue eyes looking right into his. "No. Are you going?"

"Not until you tell me to go."

*Shit*. Had he said that? He'd meant it, but had he said it? Should he have said it? Should he take it back?

"Well." Heath took a sip of his beer. Then he sank deeper into the couch, put his feet up on the coffee table and patted the couch next to him. "You better settle in then."

"Mm... I reckon I'd best."

Heath's moods moved fast as Beck's, so it must be a lawyerly thing, because his own moods were more like a mountain—they were what they were, at least until an avalanche came and changed them forever.

Heath started to giggle next to him. It started subtly, but it was definitely giggling. "That was ballsy of us, huh?"

He figured his best answer was to carefully cup said balls and pat, so gentle.

"Mm. I appreciate the care, they're tender today." Heath leaned over and gave him a quick kiss. "Is Christmas Eve a big thing for you? Or just Christmas Day? My brother and sister spend Christmas Eve with their spouses' families, and we're all together on the day."

"I used—" No. It didn't matter what he used to do. That

was over and done. "I know that Sky's babies are used to Santa coming Christmas morning early."

Heath took his hand and tangled their fingers. "The great thing about holidays is that starting new traditions can be fun. I don't mean to take you away from those kids, but you're welcome to come hang out with my looney family Christmas Day if you want to."

"I—If I'm welcome, I'd love to do both. You'll have to tell me what presents I need to get." Because that was only fair.

"No presents. Just come any time. Very casual. Teenagers, kids, dogs...it's a zoo. It's possible no one will even notice you're there." Heath laughed.

He'd buy a bottle of wine or borrow one from Beck, then. He couldn't go to a party empty-handed. He was raised better.

"If that's moving too fast, don't be polite, okay? Just say so."

"Oh, I'm not worried about meeting new folks. In fact, I'm pretty good at it." Parker grinned; he liked to meet people. He liked people, in general. He wished he was a better bull rider, and he could stand to be a hell of a lot smarter, but being friendly? That he was good at.

"You did okay with me, for sure. I don't usually have plans Christmas Eve. Sometimes I hang out with Mom, but I was thinking—" Heath shrugged. "I have a tree in a box in my garage. I've never used it. You want to...put it up?"

He grinned at Heath. "Sure, man! That sounds like so much fun. We can be all shiny and shit."

He loved Christmas and all the nonsense around it.

Heath stole a quick kiss. "Cool. I think there are ornaments and stuff? Mom sent boxes a couple of years ago, and I just never—well, anyway. Come on."

Oh, an adventure. How fun. He stood up and took a

hard, happy kiss. He wanted Heath to know how cool this was.

Maybe he'd never have his own Christmas stuff to put up, but he could help Heath find his Christmas spirit.

It was cold in the garage, and he shivered, but Heath didn't seem bothered, as usual. "It's all back here." Heath pointed to a big box with a picture of a Christmas tree on it and a bunch of other boxes piled up next to it. "I guess we should bring it all in."

"I can do that." He was small, but he was mighty, and he could haul shit with the best of them.

He bent down, grabbed two boxes, and started up the stairs, whistling "Jingle Bells".

Heath chuckled and followed him with the tree. They had everything inside in no time, and he was struck, again, by how much simpler some things were with two people. He looked around Heath's living room, which wasn't tiny, but wasn't exactly spacious.

"Where should we put it? Not close to the wood stove of course..."

"In the window." It was important, because then they could see it from the outside and it would sparkle on the snow.

"Yeah." Heath nodded and pointed to the sliding glass door that led to the deck. "In that window."

"Good deal. Let's do it." He sliced the box open with his pocketknife and started digging out the chunks of fake pine.

"Wait, we need music, right? Christmas music." Heath left him to open the box and pulled out his phone. The unmistakable strains of Mariah Carey filled the room at a pretty good volume.

And Heath sang along at the top of his lungs.

At one point, they started dancing, just moving around

the boxes and the garland, and it was like a Christmas movie.

Heath was leading and everything.

"Do you know, my mother made me take dancing classes when I was a kid. Like actually ballroom classes. I don't know what she thought I was going to be when I grew up. Funny thing is, I loved it, and it stuck with me." As if to prove his point, Heath gave him a twirl.

Oh, he loved to dance. Loved it. "I could dance for days."

Nothing made him happier.

"Days might be a bit long. We'd have to break for a pizza at least." Heath pulled him in steered him past another box.

"Mmhmm. And coffee. Coffee is important." He stole a long, lazy kiss.

This was...yeah, he was so in.

## 13

_____

A few days ago, he was just steady old Heath, with not much more going on than shoveling and work and a banister to rebuild.

Today, he had a Christmas tree, company to share his frozen pizzas, and a hot cowboy at the top of his to-do list.

Who was he?

Like really, who the hell was he?

This couldn't be real, but he was pretty sure it was.

"Earth to Heath."

He blinked at Beckett. "Oh. Sorry, I was thinking." He looked back down at his laptop and tapped a few keys to make it look like he was doing something.

"About what? You'd checked out, man."

He sighed. "I did. You're right. I think I'm... I don't know."

Beckett pushed his chair back. "You know what, we're done. I'll send the agreement off tomorrow, and then we're off until after New Year's."

"Yeah? Cool." He closed the laptop and set it aside.

"So you're what? Tired?" Beckett gave him a knowing grin.

"Did Parker—?"

"Parker told Sky."

"And Skyler—"

"Told me of course." Beckett grinned at him. "You dawg."

He shook his head. "It's not like that. I just like him."

"He's a good guy. He's amazing with the kids. What's he up to this afternoon?"

"Christmas shopping with Charlie." Parker had been texting and sending pictures.

"Again? Well, they'll be back by grill time. Lucky thing we got his truck working."

"Yeah, great timing. Although I can't say I mind him being stuck at my place." He didn't mind at all. "I'm mean, this is kind of new, you know?"

"Sure, and he's different from most guys around here..." Becket winked at him.

"Thank God for that." Parker wasn't like anyone around here. Or anyone he'd been with before, either. "He's... fucking *fun*, man."

"Yeah. Yeah, he has a hell of a sense of humor too. You coming to our house for Christmas morning, do you think? There'll be cinnamon rolls."

"I can't, but Parker will be. I've got my nephews, my niece. You know. Mom would flip. Parker might join me later. I invited him."

"Good deal. He'll be done with us by...oh...seven a.m."

"Seven? Good Lord." If that was the case, he probably could come. "He better sleep here Christmas Eve."

"Whatever you guys decide. Honestly. The kids will only be focused on Santa."

"That's gotta be fun. I remember back when my sister's

twins were little…so cute." He'd never been there for the dawn wake-up calls, but he remembered how Christmas was magic to them.

"Oh God, yes. Especially now that Charlie cares about buying presents for her sibs. It's adorable."

"I think it's good for Parker too. The shopping, the uncle time. He loves your kids."

"He does. He has never once missed a birthday. Not once. Even if he had to run home immediately after."

He did that too, but he didn't have to fly hundreds of miles to do it. "Family first."

Skyler poked his head into Beckett's home office. "Hey. You guys done? It's time to get the grill going."

Beckett beamed and stood up. "I'm on it."

"Is Parker back?"

Skyler chuckled. "Charlie conned him into buying fudge for everyone in Vermont."

"She's a girl after my own heart. Did she bring butterscotch?" He followed Beckett out of the room.

"Butterscotch. Penuche. Peanut butter. Rocky Road. Chocolate. Caramel. Vanilla. Butter pecan. Walnut."

Beckett's eyes just kept getting bigger.

"I see tummy aches in your future, buddy." He shook his head. Parker was going to be in so much trouble. "Charlie! Let me take some of that butterscotch fudge off your hands."

"It's so yummy! Uncle Parker let me taste a nibble of all of them before we bought!" She was flying.

Flying.

"Good work, Uncle Parker. You're going to be so popular with her dads." But he dug right into the fudge himself, didn't he?

"I know. It's worth it." Parker licked chocolate off his fingers.

Beckett went stomping by in his boots and coat and slipped out the back door to the deck.

Parker opened the penuche and offered him a bite. "He's good on the grill. I guess you know that."

"Actually, I didn't know that. I'd never been here for dinner until the night you showed up." He and Beckett did happy hour, and Sky would join them in Burlington for dinner sometimes, but he hadn't ever been in their house for a meal.

"No? Wild! Have you had them to yours, yet?"

"Never. We've always been go out to dinner types." He shrugged. It didn't feel weird to him; he and Beckett were colleagues. Work friends.

"That's cool. Seriously. No judgment. I don't have a house. Or an office." Parker winked at him.

"I do have a Christmas tree to show off now though. Oh —speaking of which, Beckett says their whole Christmas thing is done by like seven a.m., so I could come, and then we could head over to my mom's at like nine or ten. What do you think?"

"I love that. I found her a nice basket with goodies and wine." Parker sucked a pecan clean of fudge.

"That's totally unnecessary, and she will love it." He winked at Parker. "Thank you."

"I want them to know I'm a good guy."

Yeah, he could see how that was super important to Parker. The man traded hard on his charisma.

He bumped shoulders with Parker. "I like my housewarming gift better."

Parker tilted his head, obviously confused. "What did you get, honey?"

He lowered his voice and leaned very close to Parker. Charlie had wandered off with the chocolate marshmallow fudge, but he still didn't need anyone overhearing. "Kitchen sex. Best gift ever."

"Ooh..." Parker leaned too. "Wait for bent-over-the-sofa sex."

Parker was too much fun. "Can I make a reservation for tonight?"

Those gorgeous eyes lit up. "I am absolutely sure I have an...opening."

"Free parking?" He was really trying not to laugh.

"Oh, no. No way." Parker winked at him. "I'm pricey."

"Damn. Well, I think I have the funds, and at least I know there's no valet." There was such a thing as carrying a metaphor too far, and he was pretty sure they were there.

Parker snorted and leaned in, kissing him softly, so warm and quick.

He smiled. "The butterscotch is—"

"I saw that," Beckett said passing by them and getting a tray of steaks out of the fridge.

"The fudge is good, huh?" Butter wouldn't melt in Parker's mouth.

"Best fudge ever."

"I'm so glad you both...enjoy sweets." Beckett laughed and took the steaks back out to the deck.

"So this is an official thing then? Beckett says you're coming for Christmas morning, and then going to Heath's mom's. She's a nice lady; you'll like her." Skyler wandered in with Sierra on one hip.

Sierra reached for Parker, and Parker took her without hesitation.

"I think we're in the vicinity of thing, right, honey?"

"Well, I don't want you to leave, and you don't want to go, so I think we're some kind of thing." Heath nodded and took

Parker's hand. It seemed important to make sure Parker knew he wasn't afraid of being acknowledged.

Parker smiled at him and held on, the touch sweet and solid. "There you go. We're a thing."

Skyler's smile was wide. "Excellent. We like seeing our friends happy."

Sierra was quiet and snuggled into Parker. It was so cute, and Parker was completely comfortable with it. "You have a good day, kiddo? You getting ready for Santa?"

"Santa!"

"That's right. It's getting close."

"Tomorrow is Christmas Eve. That came up fast. We tend to lay low because Christmas Day is a bit wild around here. What are your plans?"

Heath looked at Parker and nodded. "Lay low."

Parker nodded. "Look at the pretty lights and watch Elf."

"We have a road trip after Christmas so it will be good to just chill for a while."

Sky's eyes lit up. "You're really going to get Sheila?"

Parker glanced to him, then the man nodded. "Looks like it. She's my dog."

"I'm just going to be company on the road. And backup if needed. It'll be fun. Parker is well-traveled, but I never go anywhere."

"I'll give him the goofy sh-tuff tour of the Midwest."

"Ah, Cleveland, Terre Haute, St. Louis. Lots of goofiness on that trip." Sky beamed at them, looking like a weird bobble head doll.

"Can I help with dinner? Set the table or...anything not-cooking related?" Heath shrugged. "You don't want me cooking."

"Sure. You can help Charlie. She's on table setting duties this week."

"I can't wait until you aren't worried Sierra will break the plates," she called out, and Heath swore Sierra winked.

"Your assistant is on the way!" Heath dared to give Parker a peck on the cheek. "I'll be back."

Sierra kissed Parker's other cheek and waved at Heath. "Bye!"

He waved back, and something inside him, for the very first time in his entire life whispered, "You'd be a great dad."

He'd never considered it. Never even mused about it.

And today, two days before Christmas, at the beginning of a relationship that shouldn't be feeling anything like forever yet but felt that way anyway, was not the time to listen too hard to random whispers.

But just as there were things he couldn't unsee, this was something he couldn't...unthink.

Damn.

Parker was so sweet with that little girl, though.

## 14

Parker couldn't believe it was already Christmas Eve.

He couldn't believe he was hanging out with someone he'd never even met two weeks ago.

What the hell was wrong with him?

Maybe it was Santa Claus, giving him one hell of a present.

He'd been ready for Sky and Beck to be shocked, like, how dare you meet this business associate friend and jump in bed with him? But they were weirdly cool about it. Happy even. He supposed that ought to make him feel better.

It didn't matter; this was the most fun he'd had in longer than he could remember.

Heath was the hottest motherfucker he'd ever seen.

"So what do you think?" Heath asked, walking up behind him as he looked out at the Christmas snow. "I want to build a balcony, like a nice-size deck off my bedroom because the view from that room is the best in the house."

"I think that would rock. Never made something like that, but I love the idea." And he could help. He could figure it out. He knew how to figure out shit, if he was still here.

"Well, see, but I also really want a garage. An attached one off the kitchen for...obvious reasons." He gestured to the snow. "But also somewhere to store my tools and maybe have a permanent workbench and everything. I can't decide which should be the spring project."

"Well...would the garage help the balcony building more or versy-vicey?" He thought the garage would be less cool, but more useful.

"I don't think I need a garage to build the balcony. It'll be spring and summer and all the construction would be outdoors. But then, come winter, I'd be back to working indoors, and shoveling snow off our trucks." Heath chuckled and slipped an arm around Parker. "And like this winter, I couldn't pre-build the decking for the balcony or anything." Heath sighed. "What do you think?"

"I think the garage is the smart decision, and the balcony is the yummy decision, but I think either way, it's going to be good work."

"And they'll both happen eventually." Heath sighed. "It should probably be the garage. I want the balcony, but I need the garage more. Plus, I get to hire someone to level the ground and pour concrete. How cool will that be?"

"Oh, that sounds fun as hell, and I can help. That'll save you some money." He wasn't sure of...well, anything.

"It'll be great to have help. Fun too. I'm used to doing things by myself, but this is a big project. I was anticipating hiring some people for parts of it, but you're handy. We could maybe handle it ourselves."

Heath was either more sure or more optimistic, because Heath didn't seem to have any doubts as to where he'd be come spring.

"I'm in. I love...being useful." And he had some savings, so he could help out.

"You don't have to be yet. It's Christmas Eve." Heath pulled out his phone and Nat King Cole started singing over the speakers in the living room. "Can I have this dance?"

"Oh, I would be over the moon, honey." Parker thought that he was in heaven as he moved into Heath's arms. He was tall for a bull rider, and Heath made him feel almost small.

"You said you loved to dance." Heath pulled him in with one arm around his back. "Merry Christmas."

"I do. Merry Christmas, honey." He let himself relax as he blew out a soft sigh.

"So, we don't cook, but it's Christmas Eve. Should we go pick something up?"

Parker grinned at him, because for once, he had this. "I got supper all figured, believe it or not."

"What?" Heath beamed at him. "You do?"

"I do." He had a whole tray that he'd picked up. It had cheeses and sausages, crackers and dips, pickles and olives on one side, chocolates and fruits and teeny tiny cakes on the other. And the board was wood and came with little knives and shit that stuck into the sides.

"You're sneaky." Heath danced him in a circle. "I love that. Have you decided what movies we're watching too?"

"Nope. I mean, I know I said *Elf*, I thought we could decide that together." It was going to be an amazing night— and he thought Santa might even come tonight.

"I'm happy you're here. With me. Happy isn't even the right word. Grateful maybe."

"I never even imagined someone like you. My brain isn't big enough for that, but I'm thankful you're...here." Parker was scared to be so happy.

"So tell me about retiring. About bull riding. What did

you love about it?" They were still dancing to one Christmas song after another.

"I loved the folks. I used to love dreaming about being amazing, a champ, but I figured out that wasn't in the cards, so I started focusing on making money."

Heath gave him a curious look. "But did you love riding?"

"It's literally my only skill. I liked making a living, having sponsors, but the riding? It stops being fun after the tenth broken bone."

"I bet. I feel like every time I touch you I find another scar." Heath touched one on his neck, then leaned in and kissed it.

"I hear that." Truer words probably had never been spoken, but it was okay. He was a survivor.

"It's impressive you know. I'm pretty impressed anyway. That's a lot of pain and recovery and perseverance. Not everyone could do it. In fact, I'd bet very few can." Heath traced another scar on his chin and kissed that one too.

Being in love was like riding, he was figuring out, except instead of falling and hitting the ground, Heath kept him spinning.

Heath gently untucked his shirt and slid the hand that was leading him up his back, warm fingers splaying over his spine.

"Love." He blinked up and leaned back all at once, his heart beat speeding just a touch.

"Well, it's early for dinner yet." Heath winked at him. "I was thinking I'd check out that reservation."

"Oh, honey. I'm in. All the way." He stood on tiptoe and took a hard, hungry kiss. Heath caught his ass with the other hand and tugged him in tight.

"Ever get busy under a Christmas tree? I haven't."

"I have to admit, the opportunity has never arisen." He was not in the least opposed, however.

Heath smiled at him, fingers working on his buttons. "Allow me to make an opportunity, then."

"Mmhmm..." He was all melted, but he managed to get his fingers working, didn't he?

"I wonder how many times you've visited, and I just never got a chance to meet you? It's weird right?"

His shirt slid off and Heath shrugged out of his own sweater.

"It is. Because I've been here a bunch. From the time Sky came home to the babies." He reckoned the good Lord was making him wait for the right time.

"I guess that makes more sense. I held down the fort at work during all those big events. We might have run into each other and not even realized—I helped move the kids' things into the house, delivered meals a couple of times." Heath has his jeans loose in seconds, fingers slipping under the denim and cupping his ass.

"I would have remembered you." His toes curled and his glutes went tight as hell. "I have no doubt."

"I think I would have remembered you too." Heath rocked them together, hips bumping. "I couldn't forget your eyes, your smile."

"Then we've just been orbiting around each other." He loved that idea, missing each other until it was right.

"Not anymore." Heath caught his jaw in one hand and kissed him, turning up the heat just that easily.

He pushed Heath's T-shirt up, fingers dragging on the sweet, fuzzy belly. Yum.

They'd stopped dancing and were just swaying really, and not even to the beat of whatever Heath's phone was playing. Heath backed him up to the sofa and gave him a playful push to make him sit, then knelt slowly.

He leaned forward and brought their mouths together, the kiss starting soft, but turning into a long, deep connection.

Heath was in no hurry, and they made out like kids on a first date. Just the kiss, nothing handsy. It was higher-level, though, and it felt like they were telling each other things you couldn't put words to.

He hummed, his eyelids heavy. He'd never made out like this, where they knew they had all the time in the world.

The kiss ended almost gracefully, and Heath had flushed pink, so obvious despite the beard. Heath tugged his slippers off and then went after his jeans, fingers curling into the waistband.

He loved how Heath worked to make the house warm enough for this, warm enough for him.

He never even had to ask. It was just...done.

Heath wiggled the jeans off and set them aside, then pulled the phone from his pocket and set it on the coffee table. It was still beaming music to the speakers, which were cleverly hidden somewhere in the room.

He reached out, stroking one of Heath's nipples to hardness. He loved how that made his lover gasp and groan.

Heath wasn't the only one who knew how to light a fire.

"I don't know why, but that's so good, babe." Heath pushed his knees open and slid a hand under his balls, cupping them through his briefs.

"Uh-huh." He leaned in, lips close to Heath's ear. "I've never felt anything like you make me feel. Ever."

Heath's breath caught as he inhaled and he saw the goosebumps rise up on his lover's arms. "Damn. Me either. You just have my number."

"Good." He wasn't going to bitch about that at all. No way. He nibbled on Heath's earlobe, humming deep in his chest.

"Mhm. So good." Heath leaned into the touch a bit and hot fingers slid over his shaft, toward the top of his briefs. "Santa thinks you should take these off."

He chuckled and nodded. "Never let it be said I want on the naughty list."

Then he lifted his hips and slid his briefs off, leaving himself bare as the day he was born.

"Mm. Someone's getting everything they ask for this Christmas." Heath's fingers curled firmly around his prick. "Do you have a wish list, babe?"

"I do." He wanted to stay here, with Heath, build a life.

"I bet it's pretty close to the same as mine." Heath kissed him with more heat this time, fingers stroking him.

All he could do was hope so.

He pushed closer, one leg wrapping around Heath and pulling him tighter.

Heath's kiss slipped over his chin, along his jaw and down over one shoulder to his chest. All the while that hand moved on him, slow and steady, making him buzz.

He rode it, lips parted, his entire focus on Heath's hand. Nothing had ever—Christ, he wanted this to last forever.

"Can I have a taste, babe?" Heath's lips traveled across his belly.

He groaned, his lips parted. "God, yes. Please, love. I want."

Heath didn't hesitate. A curious tongue dipped right into his slit, and Heath hummed. "Mm. Nice."

"Uhn." He meant it too. So fucking amazing.

His cock slid past Heath's lips, and that was all the coherent thought he had left. Heath licked and sucked and teased him until his toes curled, and he was sucking in breaths.

His entire world was Heath—and he was all in for it. He let himself hump up, cry out and offer himself in the best possible way.

Heath swallowed around him, throat working the head of his prick, fingers digging into his thighs.

"Gonna." He didn't want to. He wanted this to last forever.

His body wasn't listening.

Heath wasn't either. Heath's fingers slid back behind his balls, just barely touching, before gliding over his hole.

That was all he needed. His toes curled, his abs went tight, and he shot, his bones rattling with the force of it.

Heath stayed right with him until he relaxed, until he could breathe a little, then knelt up tall again, smiling with well-fucked lips. "Merry Christmas."

"Mmm...merry Christmas." He reached for Heath. "What do you need, honey?"

He'd give it over, no question.

Heath climbed up next to him, sitting close, and combed strong but gentle fingers through his hair. "Nothing right now. I'm riding a serious buzz and I love it. I'll call in my couch sex reservation in a bit."

"Mmm..." He nuzzled into the touch, his lips parted in pure bliss. "This is the best Christmas Eve ever."

"I don't know, there was this one when I was like six, and it had been snowing for days and—ow!" Heath grinned and recoiled playfully, like his little pinch had been a poke with a hot iron. "That hurt!"

"Aw...poor sweet innocent lawyer-jack..." He stroked the offended nipple with his thumb.

"Lawyer-jack?" Heath snorted. "This really is the best Christmas ever. But we have to get up so early tomorrow!"

"Mmhmm...but we can sleep all we want tomorrow evening."

"True. And then we need to get on the road, huh?"

"Are you sure?" It was a long-assed drive, and Mom was going to be a bitch about things, but damn. He wanted his dog back.

"Are you kidding? We have to go get your best friend from the clutches of a homophobe—I mean your mother."

"Yes. It's weird, huh? How you come from somebody that...is so different from you?" And such an asshole.

"I don't understand it, but then I don't come from that kind of family. How do you not love your kid more than anything? I hope you know that it's entirely her, not you." Heath stroked a hand over his chest, then reached out and grabbed a blanket, spreading it out over them both.

"It is what it is. I can't change her, and she can't change me." He snuggled in, trying not to lose the peace.

"Why would anyone want to?" Heath kissed his forehead. "You're fucking perfect."

"Maybe for you, and that's all I need, right?" He could be crappy for everyone else.

Maybe not the kiddos.

He loved them.

"Can we eat your Christmas Eve meal naked, or should I grab your clothes? We can stick them under here and warm them up."

"It's all finger foods. No need to dress." He hauled his happy ass up and went to the fridge. Two platters and a couple of beers.

It was perfect.

Heath dragged him back under the blanket as soon as he

sat down again. Always making sure he was warm. "You snuck all this in here? You're amazing. Thank you."

"I wanted us to have something decent with no work." And it did all looked amazing—colorful, tasty little bites of goodness.

The sun had gone down, and they were sitting in the glow of the Christmas tree lights. Heath slipped out of his jeans, tucked the blanket around them and raised his beer. "You're right, this is the best Christmas ever."

"Yeah." He clinked their bottles together, met Heath's eyes. "Thank you."

"Hey, don't thank me. You brought the cocktail weenies." Heath waggled his eyebrows and grabbed one.

He had snow, lights, and finger food. Next up, a movie and figuring out the best way to pay Heath back for that wild blow job.

Christmas really couldn't get any better.

## 15

Heath pulled his robe tighter around him, stoked up the wood stove, turned the thermostat up, and made coffee. It had become his morning routine. He and Parker kept each other plenty warm all night but by morning the house was chilly and his cowboy didn't really understand the cold yet.

He would, if he stayed long enough, but Parker wasn't there right now.

It was still dark so he turned on the tree before he headed back upstairs.

It was Christmas morning.

Very, very early Christmas morning.

Parker lifted the covers. "C'mere, honey. I need you to warm me up."

"I'm going to be cold, you know." He set their coffees down on the bedside table, ditched his robe and slippers and climbed back into bed. "And those kids are waiting don't forget."

"Uh-huh. Just two minutes. No more. Just two." Parker pushed right into him.

"Two minutes." He wrapped his arms around Parker. He could stay here for many more minutes. "Merry Christmas."

"Merry Christmas." Parker rubbed their noses together. "The coffee smells good."

"It's hot. To warm up my cowboy."

"You're too good to me." Parker held him tight. "I'll warm up my lawyer."

"Is this a hard day for you? Where do you usually spend Christmas, babe?"

"Mom's, usually." Parker wrinkled his nose. "I run down, stay for the day, and run away."

"So...this is better. You don't miss it?"

"God no. I...you...you make things... amazing."

"Good. I want you to be happy. Especially today." Heath snorted. "I must really care about you to get my ass out of bed this early today, right?"

"You really must care about those babies, too."

"I do. I knew their biological parents, and Skyler and Beckett's house has so much love in it." He thought maybe he was a little jealous, though he never had been before.

"It does." Parker stole a kiss. "So does yours."

"Lately, that's true." He'd put a lot of care into the house too, but that wasn't the same.

"I'm glad. I hope you can say the same thing next Christmas."

"I really hope so too." He had no doubt, but did he dare say that out loud? He wasn't going anywhere. "I figure if we can survive a road trip together, we can survive anything."

"I have spent my entire adult life on the road, honey." Parker cupped his cheek. "Once this trip is over, I'd like to set my burden down some."

"Good. You and Sheila will settle right here then." He

kissed Parker and whispered, "You can be the foreman on our garage project."

The "our" was important to him.

"I can." Parker didn't seem worried in the least. "I'm a smart dog. I'll learn to fit in here and be...irreplaceable."

"You're not going to have to try very hard." He kissed Parker again. The one thing neither of them was ever going to have to work on was wanting each other. "Damn." He pulled back suddenly. "Can't disappoint the kids."

"No. No, Santa would be mad." Parker's eyes were laser focused. "Come on, gorgeous. Let's do this. If we stay in here, I'll get busy."

"Promises, promises." He slid out of bed and found Parker's robe and tossed it to him before pulling his own back on. The house was warming up, but it wasn't as warm as Parker liked it yet.

"It is. I will pay up when we get home today." Parker kissed his nose. "I promise."

"Holding you to that." He ducked into the bathroom and started the shower so the bathroom would warm up. "Mom is excited to meet you."

"I'm excited too. Moms like me." There was no doubt in Parker's voice.

"Yeah? You're good at sucking up to your boyfriends' mothers?" He held the shower door for Parker and followed him in. Somehow, they managed to stay all business as they cleaned up.

"Hey! I'm a cowboy—we're polite, friendly, good to ladies and children, and I come bearing gifts." Parker winked at him, wiggling happily.

"Oh, right. You're not like us Yankee assholes; I forgot." Heath gave him a toothy grin.

"I happen to be deep into a certain Yankee, so I'll thank you not to abuse him." Parker blew him a kiss.

He laughed and shut the water off. "All clean. And not feeling abused in the least." He ducked out and grabbed towels. "Mom keeps her house warm, so wear layers." He always ended up in a T-shirt by dinner time.

"Got it."

Parker dressed quickly in his button-down, covered with a flannel. "This way I can show up with no stains."

"So clever. You look good in flannel." He kissed Parker's cheek, then took a big swallow of his coffee. "What else do we need?"

"Everything's in the truck. I just need my wallet and the wine."

"You mean this?" He snagged the wallet, waved it at Parker, and took off down the stairs.

Parker's laugh followed him, happy and warm, his lover chasing him through the house. He gave up in the mudroom after Parker cornered him there. "No fair, I have to put on boots." Heath held it up in the air out of Parker's reach.

Parker cupped his balls, rolled them, the touch firm, but not painful.

Oh, that...felt great, dammit. But no. Christmas. Kids. "Cheater! You cheat. That's cheating!"

"Nope. Love and war, right?"

"I will get you back." He handed the wallet over and bent to tug his boots on. "When you least expect it."

"Ooh. I like that. You do know how to make a guy shivery."

"I'm sure that's the draft. Get your boots on cowboy." He grabbed his keys and tried to remote-start his truck. It had gotten the time of year where it was iffy whether it would work, but it did. "Woo! Heated seats await us."

"Hell yeah. Let's go see Santa!" Parker's excitement was a little contagious. He bounced along a little like Pepe Le Pew.

They sang loudly with a holiday playlist all the way to Beckett and Skyler's house, and the sun was just starting to come up as they arrived.

It was still so damn early.

Charlie was on the front porch, though, fully dressed, staring. "Uncle Parker! Uncle Heath! Santa came!"

"Of course he did." Parker beamed and slid out of the truck. "Happy Christmas!"

She waited long enough for Parker to reach the porch and then hung on him all the way inside. "It's *Merry* Christmas, silly."

"Oh, sorry. Merry Christmas, sweetie. I love y'all so much."

"Good morning, guys. Coffee?"

He nodded. "Yes, please."

"Uncle Parker!" Noah came running and launched himself into Parker's arms. "I was a good boy, and Santa came!"

"I told you, didn't I? You are amazing!" Parker spun Noah around.

"You did! I am amazing!" Noah clapped his hands.

That made him laugh. "And the volume level for this hour of the morning is amazing too."

"Don't be a humbug, Scrooge." Beckett clapped him on the shoulder. "Coffee."

"Oh, thank you." Maybe he could handle things now.

Sierra came squealing in, and suddenly Parker was surrounded by children. Parker plopped down on the floor in front of the tree with all of them, oohing and aahing like Santa had actually shown in the flesh.

"A dog isn't going to be enough for him," Beckett whispered.

He raised an eyebrow. "What does that mean?"

Beckett pointed. "Kids."

"Dude. We've known each other a week."

"I know." Beckett walked away laughing. "Who's ready to open a present?"

"Me!" The kids went nuts, and Parker helped to get them all settled.

You don't say, "How do you feel about kids," after a week. Especially if you don't know yourself. Not that he needed to ask that question, anyone with eyes could see that Parker was destined to be a dad.

"One thing at a time," he said out loud to no one in particular.

"Santa came for you too, Heath." Parker leaned down to whisper in Sierra's ear, and she stood, running over to take his hand.

"Uncle! Come *on!*"

"Oh my goodness." He held her little hand and let her lead him to a spot on the floor near Parker. Then she plopped right down in his lap. "Oh. Hi."

Skyler chuckled somewhere behind him.

"Santa came for you too! Look!"

There were, in fact, a lovely little set of presents, all marked "To Heath, From Santa."

He recognized Parker's wrapping paper on most of them.

He had presents too, but they were at Mom's, so Parker would just have to wait.

"Santa came for me? I guess I was a good boy."

Sierra smiled up at him. "Pappy says you're very nice."

He was surprised Beckett talked about him. "He does? Do you think I'm nice?"

Sierra nodded. "You're nice, and you have a neat beard."

"Well, thank you, sweetheart." He glanced at Parker. "I heard Santa came for you at my Mom's house."

"Ooh. I get two Santa visits. You know what that means?"

Noah nodded. "That lots of people love you."

"That's right. I'm so glad to be home, y'all. Finally."

Finally.

He wondered if Parker knew he felt that way too.

P arker checked his shirt, made sure everything was in order with no stains. Then he made sure his belt was appropriately shiny and his boots were nice. He'd never had to meet a mama of somebody he cared about.

He'd met Beckett's momma and daddy, of course.

And he liked Beckett.

But he'd never met the momma of somebody he was in an "I know what your balls smell like" sort of relationship with.

Still, he knew how to be nice, how to smile, and he loved Heath. These were the folks who had raised Heath up.

Heath took his hand and kissed his fingers. "You're beautiful. They're going to love you; you said so yourself. Ready?"

"I am." He grabbed the presents, scooping them up in his arms, leaving the wine to last. "Let's do this thing."

Heath closed the truck doors since his hands were full and followed him up to the house. It was a cute little townhouse with lots of light coming from the windows to offset the gray day. The door opened before they made it to the porch. "It's about time. I almost had to open a beer alone."

"Logan!" Heath jogged up and gave the guy a hug. They were both solid and the hug was real, not one of those bro hug deals. "Parker, this is my baby brother Logan."

"Aw, man. You are so welcome. Heath never brings anybody to these things. This is great. Can I help?" Logan held his hands out for presents.

"Absolutely! Pleased to meet you, sir. I'm Parker." He held out one hand for a kind of awkward little shake and then handed over some presents. "Nice place you got here."

Cold as fuck, but nice and snowy, which was perfect for Christmas.

Not nervous. He was not nervous.

"Isn't it cute? It's Mom's. I'm sure Heath told you." Logan held the door open and a lot of warm air and sound greeted him. Christmas music, people chatting. laughter.

"Logan, where's my beer? Did you get lost—oh! Heath!"

"Hey, guys!" The town house had a nice open floor plan, and it was full of people. "Everyone, this is Parker."

They greeted him cheerfully and loudly, and he got hugs from Heath's big sister and Logan's wife on the way across the room to where Heath's mom was hanging out with a little girl who had to be Heath's niece.

"Parker Stephens, this is my mother, Margaret Wooledge, and my niece, Opal."

"Goodness, that was formal." Margaret got to her feet and gave him a smile. "Peggy, please. So good to meet you, Parker."

"Yes, ma'am. I'm tickled as all get out to meet you as well." He held out one hand. "I've heard a lot of good things."

"They're all lies. I'm an evil, ornery old woman." She

took his hand and covered it with her other one. "You are very welcome here. Just don't ever take the last slice of pie." She winked at him.

"I would never." He knew better. He was nothing if not polite. "You have my word, ma'am."

Heath laughed. "But if she hands it to you, you will eat it. She doesn't care if you're full."

"Now, Heath."

"It's true, Mom."

Peggy squinted and gave him a naughty smile. "It is kind of true."

Opal was quiet and hid behind her grandmother a bit, so he just gave her a little wave. She waved back.

They were all suddenly dwarfed by two tall teenagers who looked practically interchangeable. "Hey, Uncle Heath."

"Hey there, boys." Heath dropped his voice into a low register to tease them about their own low voices.

"Yeah, yeah. We're still taller."

"You will always be taller."

One of the twins looked at him. "You ride bulls, right?"

"Like Sky?"

Sixteen and still finishing each other's sentences.

"Yes, sirs, but Sky's the champ. Always will be." He was just a cowboy who rode bulls.

"That's so tough."

"Seriously cool."

"This is Hayes and Tate, they belong to Keira and Doug. And over there are Levi and Warren, Opal's big brothers."

"Good to meet y'all. Thanks for letting me crash the party." He was never going to remember all these names.

"Mom, Parker brought presents and wine." Heath's sister

slid in next to him. "I'm Keira. This will all calm down in a bit. Can we open that?"

"Absolutely. I brought a couple of bottles. I knew there would be a lot of folks." And wine was a good, safe, generous gift.

At least that was what Sky said.

"Of course he did. I can tell already he was raised well."

Heath got pulled away by one of his nephews and shot him a grin and a wave.

Keira took the bottle. "Would you like a glass? Or a beer? Or soda? It's never too early on Christmas."

"I'll take a Coke—whatever y'all have."

"A Coke. We have that." Keira took him literally, which he probably should have figured she would.

"I've been a teetotaler my whole life," Peggy said, giving him a nod. "Good for you."

He smiled, winking over—all the while cursing Heath the littlest bit. "I've been known to have a drink or two, but it's a little early for me."

Peggy patted his arm. "No judgment from me, dear."

"Parker!" Heath picked his way around people and presents to get back to him. "Mom, can I steal him?"

"Of course. I was just going to sit."

Heath beamed at him and pulled him toward a quieter end of the living room. "Sorry, the nephews got me. Did you want a beer? It's kind of a tradition to start early around here."

"I'll finish the Coke and then have one. Remember, I'm what? Half your size?" He couldn't begin to keep up.

"Maybe three-quarters." Heath and his brother were built big. Keira's husband was more like him, leaner and lighter. "Is this too much for you? You good?"

"I'm great. It's a big, happy family. I fit right in." Parker winked at Heath, admiring his lumberjack-lawyer.

"You fit great." Heath tucked an arm around his waist. "I'm really glad you're here."

"Thank you. I am too—I want to celebrate with you, honey." He wanted to enjoy this Christmas, for the first time in a long time.

"Well, let's start with your presents." Heath pulled a small box wrapped in newspaper from his pocket. "I didn't have any Christmas paper, sorry."

"No worries." He unrolled the newspaper and opened the box, finding a gorgeous leather keychain, a single key attached to it. "Oh."

Oh damn. This was...amazing.

"It isn't really home if you can't come and go as you please."

"Thank you." It was the best gift he'd ever gotten. He looked around, making sure no one was looking, and then he kissed Heath good and hard.

Heath laughed as they parted. "You're welcome." Heath kept an arm around him. "Mom likes you. You were right. She doesn't tease and joke with people she doesn't like."

"Oh good. I'm glad." He tended to be safe on the mother front, but there was no way to tell.

"Look at you two standing over here like a couple of wallflowers." That was uh—the brother-in-law. Uh—

Heath helped him out. "How've you been, Doug?"

*Doug.*

"Good. Busy." Doug looked at him. "And believe me, I get it. I remember my first Christmas, and Logan wasn't even married yet. It's all good. Also sometimes awkward, but good. I promise."

"I am having a great holiday." And there was no lie there. None.

"So you're taking a holiday break from bull riding I hear? The boys were excited to meet you. I guess they found you online."

Everyone had gotten the bull rider memo, but it seemed like no one knew or cared that he and Heath had only known each other a whole week.

"I'm totally on a good break, yes." He was hoping for a nice long, long break, in fact.

"Well deserved, I'm sure. Hope you're hungry. Peggy doesn't believe in diets."

Heath snorted. "Parker eats like I do."

"Oh. Well, then we'll be rolling you both out of here together later."

He wasn't a dieter. He was always hungry, and he probably always would be. "I'm game. It all smells amazing."

"Avoid the fruitcake. It's...heavy."

"If it comes up, just tell Mom how amazing her potatoes are. Which they are. She'll be happy."

"The potatoes." Doug rolled his eyes blissfully. "I seriously could make a whole meal out of them with the gravy."

"So Doug is the guy we're going to call about the concrete for the garage."

"Okay! You decided? Garage first?"

"Garage first."

"Excellent. I can't wait to get started. It's going to be amazing."

Parker thought so too. A covered garage was going to be stunning.

"Doug does paving—"

"Paving and concrete. Roads, driveways, steps, foundations, whatever."

"Doug is handy. Logan is handy too, but not with tools. He's a chef. He works at a restaurant in Burlington. He actually has to go to work at four."

"Oh, that's awful, to have to go in on Christmas!" Parker knew first responders had to do it, but...damn.

"Next year he'll have enough seniority to get Christmas off. But they're busy all day today. He did get last night off, which is good for the kids."

"Keira is also a lawyer, but she's not practicing anymore. She stayed at home when we had the twins and then bought out her favorite bookstore in town, and she runs that now. Pretty cool." Doug was obviously proud.

"Oh, how fun! I've never known anyone who owned a bookstore. That's cool."

"Right? She is living her dream. It's good. The boys are driving and living their own lives now, they'll head off to college soon."

"Old fart," Heath teased.

"You better catch up, bro," Doug shot right back. "You're *way* behind."

Heath suddenly looked...constipated.

Oh, maybe this was a sore spot.

"Yeah, yeah. Go have another beer."

"I just might." Doug gave Heath a clap on the shoulder, then gave him a nod before heading for the kitchen.

"Sorry." Heath sighed. "I get that a lot."

"Why be sorry? You're all right. I promise not to catch pregnant."

"Ha." Heath shook his head. "It's not even that. They just like to tease me. I'd be okay if you did."

"Caught pregnant? That would get us in the news, for

sure." He was totally into the idea of being a dad one day, though. Maybe in three or four years.

Heath giggled and shook his head. "This family in the news? That would be all I need. They're crazy."

"Rodeo cowboy suddenly finds himself with child. News at eight." Parker cracked himself up.

"Why are you laughing?" One of the younger boys squinted up at him from under a Santa hat.

"Your Uncle Heath made a joke." He winked. "What's your favorite joke?"

"Uh... What kind of key unlocks a banana?"

Heath raised his hand. "Call on me!"

"No. You know this one, that's cheating."

Heath put his hand down. "Right. You are right."

He knew it too, but that wasn't any fun. "Hrm...a house key? No. A mouse key? No. A car key? No..."

"A mon-key!" The kid looked pleased with himself. "Monkey monkey monkey."

"Oh dude! A monkey. I love it. I'm going to remember that one."

"This is Warren. He's...ten? Yes. You're ten."

"Almost eleven."

Heath rolled his eyes. "You have eight months."

"That's almost!"

"Dude, are you a sports guy? A gamer guy?"

"I ski. Do you ski? I'm really good." Warren poked the phone in Heath's pocket. "Show him, Uncle Heath."

"Ah, yes. One second..." Heath scrolled and opened a video of Warren racing downhill.

"Oh wow. Wow, the video of me skiing is *way* less impressive." He was sort of like a cowboy snowball...

"Well, yours was impressive for other reasons."

"I'm going to the Olympics! One day."

Heath nodded. "I'm waiting and watching, kiddo."

"Anyone shorter than I am needs to come help me set the table," Heath's sister called from the kitchen door.

Heath cracked up. "That usually means the younger kids but..."

"Ooh...you're in trouble." Parker goosed his lover.

"Ow!" Heath yelped and batted at his hand. "Polite company."

"Uh-huh. I bet no one will tell on me..." He winked at Warren. "Right?"

"Tell what? I have to go set the table!" Warren took off for the kitchen.

"No fair." Heath pouted, lip protruding past his beard.

"See? Families like me. So much."

"Uh-huh." Heath pointed to the coffee table. "There's cheese." And fruit and little muffins and some nuts. "Let's get some while the kids are busy."

"Sounds great. I love these little munchies." Which Heath should remember from last night.

"How long are you in town, Parker?" Logan looked like he'd been awake almost as long as they had.

"As long as Heath keeps me." Oh, maybe he shouldn't have said that...

"Oh, Jesus. Heath is a packrat. You're here forever." Logan gave him a wink.

Heath didn't shy away from the conversation. "It's true. If I like something I hold onto it."

Logan smiled. "I knew it. You never bring anyone home. I knew it was a big deal."

"I can handle it, being his big deal." Parker popped a piece of cheese in his mouth to shut himself up.

"Seems like he fits right in." Logan stuffed a square of cheddar in his mouth.

Heath took his hand. "He knew he would, too. He's good with people."

"Mom likes him, so you're golden."

He liked that idea, being Heath's gold.

———

HEATH SAT BACK, rested his arm across Parker's chair and drew lazy circles on Parker's shoulder with his thumb. Every year he ate too much, swore he wouldn't do that again, and then did it again the next year. He was stuffed.

"Mom, dinner was outstanding as usual."

"Thank you. Keira and Pam were lifesavers this year. Oh, and Doug handled the turkey."

He and Logan exchanged glances and grins, clearly being the useless ones in the family. They knew what their job was, and it hadn't started yet.

Dishes.

So many dishes.

"Thank you, everybody."

"I don't think Parker is groaning enough over there." Logan pointed at Parker. "Does he need more pie?"

"I do not need more pie, but it was amazing." Parker looked a little like a python who'd swallowed a sheep.

"Nobody needs more pie." Heath laughed, and then looked at Logan.

"Are we ready?"

"No." Logan protested. "One more minute."

"When are you heading out on your road trip?"

"Not sure, Mom. Tomorrow sometime, when we can breathe again." He assumed it would be early-early, but he didn't want to commit to anything.

"I can't wait to meet your dog." Mom was looking tired,

but she was game to keep talking. "It's been a while since we had a dog in the family."

"Thank you. I...it means a lot to me, to be able to have her back with me." Parker seemed a little shell-shocked, to be honest.

"And we get a road trip together." Heath shifted his arm from the back of the chair to Parker's shoulders. "That will be fun."

"Car snacks!" Keira looked excited. "The best part of a road trip. Send pictures."

"Oh, I will." He would take plenty.

"I can't even think about car snacks right now, but tomorrow? Tomorrow, I'll be able to." Parker's grin was pure evil.

"I'll make you a couple of turkey sandwiches for the trip." Mom was never too tired to make sure everyone was fed.

"Thanks, Mom. That would be great." He pushed his chair back. "I think it's that time, man."

Logan nodded. "Yep. I'm coming."

When neither of them got up, everyone laughed.

Parker, though he did get up, heading straight for the kitchen like he knew exactly what the plan was.

Mom looked at him, arched an eyebrow. "I suggest you keep this one."

He laughed and hauled his butt out of his chair. "Hey, Park! You're making me look bad, man!"

Logan snorted. "Leave it you to bring home an overachiever."

"He rides bulls. Overachiever doesn't begin to describe him."

"You'll find, honey, that I am an experienced dishwasher. I have been tasked with this job more than I can say."

"Then we're going to have this kitchen cleaned up in no time." He snuck a quick kiss. "Logan will clear the table, everyone else will put the kids to bed. Mom will make sandwiches. It's a tradition."

"Rock on. Let's do this thing." Parker smiled at him, and it was like heaven. He didn't like to take credit for much, but that smile was for him. Parker hadn't been smiling when he first arrived. Not at all.

It had been a week, but somehow, they'd managed to make their time...work.

It didn't make sense.

Maybe it didn't have to.

Whenever he talked with his mom about everyone getting married and having kids, she'd say, when you know, you know. He felt like he knew, and even if he was wrong, he and Parker were having a great time, and he was going with it.

He bumped shoulders with Parker. "You want to wash or dry?"

"Wash. Duh," Parker rolled his eyes.

They goofed around, powering through the dishes while Logan cleared the table and Mom and Keira made sandwiches and put leftovers away. Everyone else was off tucking in kids or dozing off the food coma in the den.

"I've got four sandwiches and some chips ready for you boys for your trip." Mom took off her apron. "And now I'm pooped! What a wonderful day."

"Thank you for letting me come and spend the day, ma'am. It's been amazing." Parker didn't even sound at all as if he didn't mean it.

"It has, hasn't it?" Mom took the towel out of Parker's hands so she could hold them. "You have been a lovely addition. Truly. You're welcome any time."

"Thank you. He's amazing, you know. Heath. Magical."

He was not going to blush. Or that's what he told himself. It didn't work.

"Thank you, I do know. He's my boy. And he's done well for himself." Mom winked at Parker, then let his hands go. "Good luck with the road trip. Stay in touch."

They both got hugs, and then Mom took herself off to bed.

"Guess that's our cue. Look at these sandwiches. Wow." Mom didn't skimp on the turkey.

"Damn. We can eat them for days." Parker winked and helped him pack them up.

"Probably good. It's a long drive, or I assume it is. Where are we going again?" Heath laughed.

"Near Enid, Oklahoma. It's about a twenty-five-hour drive, give or take." Parker chuckled at him, shook his head. "You'll get to see the American Midwest."

Oklahoma. Wow. Well, that was what a road trip was about right? Going random places and seeing random things. "Hey, I've never been to Oklahoma. We're not driving straight through, though, right?"

"Nope. That's harsh. We'll head down the middle and up closer to the coast. We have time, right?"

"We have a week, plus a day or so. Plenty of time to wander." Heath took the bag of food. "Should we head home?"

"Sounds good to me." Parker was relaxed and easy, humming Silent Night softly.

The teenagers were watching something on TV with the volume down low, and his siblings were cleaning and packing up presents.

"We're going to say goodnight, you guys."

"I guess it's about that time, bro." Logan gave him a hug, and then everyone started hugging and saying thanks yous.

"Do you hug?" Logan opened his arms for Parker, and it was so cute.

"I do. I'm totally a hugger." Parker hugged his brother tight.

"So good to meet you. You fit right in. I'm happy for you guys."

"I am too. He's...special." Parker glanced at him. "Very."

He smiled back at Parker, then gave a wave. "Merry Christmas, everybody."

"Merry Christmas. Bye! Drive safe!"

He closed the door and everything went quiet. It was cold, and the sky was clear.

"Merry Christmas, honey." Parker hooked their arms together. "Thank you for this."

"Merry Christmas, babe. What a day, huh?" He kissed Parker's cheek. "I hope they weren't too crazy for you."

"No, they made me feel welcome. Thank you. I had a ball." Parker leaned into him. "I hope they liked me too."

"They loved you. You're part of the family now." The idea of bringing anyone home had always made him too nervous, but Parker was different.

Everything about this was different, and he thought maybe that was one of the reasons it was working so well.

"I'm glad. I want to be a part of something bigger than me." Parker beamed at him. "Let's go home. Tomorrow we start our big road trip. Together."

## 17

B eing on the road with Heath was easy, really.
It would be fabulous if they weren't going to see Mother, but it was still pretty damn easy. They had snacks, and they both liked driving.

He had tons of audiobooks and playlists, podcasts, and recordings of comedians. They could be entertained for days.

The best part was the weird roadside stuff.

They stopped for all of them—stands and stores, weird things that they needed to take their picture with, even one strange-assed little carnival with one roller coast and a fun house, all dressed in lights and fake snow.

He glanced over at Heath, smiled. "You holler when you've found a hotel for the night, and we can put it in the GPS."

"I'm looking for something fun. Like, haunted, or somebody famous was murdered there, something like that. But we may have to settle for a Holiday Inn." It was his turn to drive, Heath was scrolling and munching on a pretzel rod.

"Oh, haunted is good, but I like free breakfast too, and

Holiday Inns have those pancake machines." He was pretty easy, really.

"We are so food motivated." Heath rested a hand on his thigh. "We're getting closer. How are you feeling?"

"Nervous. I don't like being mean. It don't come natural to me." But he was fixin' to have to.

"It's not mean to pick up your own dog. Are we getting anything else? Your trailer? Or just things out of it?"

"It's mine... I mean, Sky gave it to me. She didn't pay for it." And it was in good shape. "We could camp in it."

"That would be fun." Heath went back to his phone. "Holiday Inn then, easy and pancakes. And we'll get off the road sooner. Next exit."

"Do you like camping?" Heath seemed outdoorsy, and making love out in the boonies would be fun as hell.

"Honestly, I haven't done it much. I did some tent camping for a couple of days with Logan years ago. It was mostly beer and fishing and a lot of dozing off in the sun. I'd love to try it again with you."

"This is cool, because there's a toilet and a bed with a real mattress. It's a nice set up." He had lived in it for years now, and he loved it.

"Damn. A real bed? Vacation here we come!" Heath laughed. "I can't wait to see it. We won't need a hotels on the way home! Turn left up here."

"Left. I'm on it." He merged and slid onto the off-ramp. "Assuming she hasn't sold it, but I don't know how she could without me signing."

"She can't. Technically. Don't stress that, I'm sure it's sitting there waiting for you." Heath looked out the window. "Not a lot snow here. Weird."

"No, sometimes the Midwest is snowy, sometimes not, but the cold always seems intense to me."

"We can run from the parking lot. I'll warm you up in the hotel room. Promise." Heath pointed. "See the sign?"

"I do. You make some good promises, too. I do love a good warm up." He headed straight for the green lit up sign.

He parked, and they tried not to freeze as they grabbed their bags and jogged inside. There was free coffee in the lobby, and Heath got them each a cup while he checked them into their room.

"We have cookies too," the lady behind the desk offered, so he took two.

"Cookies? Right on. Thank you." Heath joined him and they made their way to the elevator. "Tired?"

"Of driving, a bit. In general? No, I'm good." He wanted some time sitting and a long shower for sure, maybe one with Heath...

"Good. I'm hoping for—" Heath lowered his voice. "Hoping for a snuggle."

"Mmm...hell yes. A snuggle. A shower. A long lazy night in bed."

Heath waited for him to let them into their room and kissed him as soon as the door closed. "I don't know why I always want to kiss you the most when I really shouldn't, but that was the longest elevator ride of my life."

Parker went to Heath, pushing him back against the door, deepening the kiss.

Heath pulled him in by the hips and rocked them together.

Oh, hell yes. He did like that. Heath was the most solid, strong lover he'd ever had.

"Move." Heath muscled him away from the door easily, and clothing started flying.

"Mmm..." He loved this part. He got his boots off and then started helping.

Helping was super important, right?

He started in on Heath as soon as his socks were off.

"You and those damn boots." Heath growled impatiently. The way Heath's hands were on him wasn't making it easy for him to work.

"You love my boots." He got Heath's belt buckle loosened and started in on the buttons.

"I love *you*. You come with boots." Heath let a little grin slip, then one hand tucked tightly around his ass cheek.

"Fuck yeah." He let himself feel that, in his bones. "I love you, and I intend that you come in me."

"Fuck yeah. We're so good for each other." Heath picked him up and dropped him on the bed, then finished undressing himself.

He wiggled out of his undershirt and briefs, settling himself so he could watch.

Heath was so fucking fuzzy. He was this northern mountain man, all furred up for winter.

Parker licked his lips, his cock hard as nails. "Jesus, you're beautiful."

Heath climbed onto the bed, crawling toward him. "Not everyone has a lawyer-jack at their disposal."

"Just me, and I need you like breathing." He'd say not everyone had a cowboy, but they were common.

"All damn day." Heath caught him by the nape and lifted him into a hard kiss.

He opened up, hands wrapping around Heath's ass and squeezing hard. "Dammit," Heath swore, breathing hard, face already flushing pink. "Which bag is the stuff in?"

"My ditty bag, in my backpack." Slick and condoms both were waiting for them.

"On it." Heath disappeared and returned with lightning

speed, dropping condoms and lube on the bed next to him. "See? Now where was I?"

"Being the hottest motherfucker I've ever seen?" He was sure that was it.

"Right! About to fuck the prettiest cowboy on the planet." Heath was quick to use the lube and offer him slick fingers. They pressed firmly against him, insisting more than asking.

He spread, knees bent, toes curling, giving Heath total access.

Heath inhaled sharply and those two fingers slipped slowly inside him. "So hot. God, babe." The look on Heath's face was intense, so focused, all about him.

"Uh-huh. Love this. So fucking hot." His eyes rolled, and he bore down, begging for more.

Deeper.

Harder.

"Never wanted anyone like I want you, babe." Heath caught his own cock and stroked his slowly.

"Good. I'm so caught up in you." His eyes crossed.

"Fuck I can't wait... I need..." Heath took a breath and fumbled for a condom.

"Uh-huh." He tried to help, but he was a little fumble fingered.

"Uh-huh." Heath was over him in a second, thick prick pressing carefully but deliberately into him. "Fuck, yes."

Parker opened, the burn as Heath's heavy prick speared him enough to force a soft, satisfied groan from his lips.

"You're a dream. I don't know how this is real." Heath started rocking him, thrusts growing deep and strong, heavy breaths punctuating every move.

"I can feel every inch. You're fucking real." And he was all in. "Don't stop, honey."

Heath heard him and nodded, grunting every so often with the effort. Heath's face was flushed, and those eyes were trained on him, watching, focused entirely on him.

His heart pounded, and he sucked air, his entire focus on the deep stretch inside him, the perfect slide and drive.

"Baby, so good." Heath arched a bit, changing the angle just right, pegging that sweet spot like he knew exactly what he was doing.

"Heath!" He arched, his heels digging into the mattress as his balls drew up.

"Right with you, baby. Right here with you." Heath ducked his head and drew in a harsh breath. He could feel his lover starting to tremble.

"Uh-huh." That was the best he had. He was aching and fixin' to shoot his load.

"Need you. You first." Heath's voice was rough, blown. "Please, Parker."

Parker nodded, rolling his hips so that sweet prick nudged him just right. Oh, that was it.

Right fucking there.

He let himself shoot, his cry shaped like Heath's name.

"Jesus Fff—!" Heath drew out that F and then came so hard he shuddered, face going beet-colored for a second. "Fuck. Holy fuck." Heath kissed him roughly, sloppily.

"Uhn." That was close to the ode he wanted to sing to Heath, right?

Heath sighed and flopped beside him, equally eloquent. "Uh-huh."

He blinked, telling himself he couldn't just fall asleep, dammit.

Heath's fingers tangled with his and held on. "Love you."

"Love you too." He was pretty sure that was what he said.

Heath rolled out of bed, the bathroom light turned on

and water ran for a second and then Heath was back again. Heath tucked an arm under him and pulled him in for one of their epic snuggles.

"Nap, maybe? Words later. And food."

"Mmm..." He tugged the blankets up and over them. That sounded perfect.

## 18

It was Heath's turn to drive Parker's truck, which was good because the closer they got to Parker's hometown, the more anxiety he felt coming from the passenger seat.

He was sort of afraid to say anything, so he reached over and rested a hand on Parker's thigh.

The muscle there was rock hard, almost shaking with tension. Damn.

That was less than good.

Okay. He had to say something to break the tension. "It's an errand. We're there for one reason. You can do this, babe. I've got your back."

"I know. I hate that I'm going to hurt her feelings, but it's time to get my little girl."

"Parker. Love. She threw you out and told you not to come back. She has no feelings you need to care about."

"Right. Right." Parker took a deep breath. "It's hard, because she's my mom, you know?"

"I've never had family that were like this, but it has to be hard. She's always going to be your mom even...with all of this."

"Yes, but... I didn't deserve this. I was a good son." Parker's lips went tight. "I *am* a good son."

"I will be more than happy to tell her so." In fact, he planned on it. He just didn't know whether it was going to be a discussion or a parting shot.

"We're getting close. There's the trailer."

Jesus, the thing was massive, like a giant mobile hotel.

They were going to have so much fun.

"Holy shit, Parker. It's a penthouse on wheels!" He turned in, following the driveway, which felt more like an unpaved road.

"Yeah. Sky gave it to me, so it was top of the line ten years ago, and I've loved it."

"Wild. That's a nice gift. I'm surprised he didn't want it for him and Beckett." How long was this driveway?

"He and Beckett weren't quite back together. I don't know that Beckett thought he was going to walk again, by that point."

"Oh. Damn. Well, that makes more sense. Sad, but it makes sense." He looked around. "Okay, seriously. This is a driveway?"

"Yeah. The house is about three acres in. She's having a fire. I can see the smoke."

"Are you okay?" He took Parker's hand. "What are you going to say? Do you know?"

"I'll start by hooking up the trailer. That will take the longest, then I'll pick up my little girl."

So... Parker didn't plan on saying anything. That was... one way of handling it.

So if someone needed to say something, it could be him. That was fine. He would take that hit for his man.

"She's going to play the dotty old lady card. She's not old. She's not senile. She's just mean, okay?"

He nodded. "Total helpless act. I got it."

"Yeah. Flutter-flutter-I'm so Southern and a little dumb-you love me right?"

God, that was funny.

"I take it that's just for strangers."

"Yeah. Ask her neighbors. They hate her." Parker glanced at him. "Don't tell Sky how bad it gets, okay? He'll be mad."

He glanced at Parker. "Mad? You mean at her, I hope."

"Some, but mostly at me, because I never told him about how she was."

"Okay. I won't volunteer anything, but if he asks me a direct question, I'm a terrible liar." How awful was this woman?

"Fair enough. You don't have to lie. That's part of your charm."

He rolled his eyes. "Charmingly truthful?" Parker's mom might not care for his truth. "What's her name?"

"Lily. Lillian is her given name." Parker seemed like the name tasted bad.

He nodded and chose not to repeat it. "Got it. Oh. I see the house there."

Smoke poured from the chimney, there were no holiday decorations, and it seemed...gloomy.

Okay, now he was a little nervous too. Thankfully Parker said she was overly sweet so she probably wouldn't come to the door with a shotgun. "So...dog first and then we go back to the camper?"

"Back the truck up to the camper. I can attach pretty damn quick." Parker grinned at him. "Don't worry. I have the paperwork in the glove compartment, and the sheriff knows me. If she calls him and he comes out, we should be solid."

"You got it." Sheriff. Jesus Christ. He was starting to understand why Parker was just going to let the camper and his dog go.

Still. He was a big guy, he was in good shape, and he would handle this. For Parker, he'd do just about anything.

They backed up to the trailer, and he'd just gotten the truck close when the door to the house opened.

The woman who stood there didn't look like she'd be scary at all. A little roundish lady in jeans and a sweatshirt, her brown hair up in a messy bun—she looked like a mother.

Oh boy. *Pure evil in a tiny mom-shaped package*, he reminded himself. He took a breath. "Here we go." He gave Parker's hand a squeeze, then climbed out of the truck.

"Parker."

"Hey, Momma. Came to get Sheila and my shit. Did you have a good Christmas?" Parker smiled, the expression false and utterly icy.

"You're not welcome here."

"No? Shame. I'll be out of your hair in ten." He whistled sharp and loud, and a tiny little brown ball of fur hurtled out of the house.

"No! She's mine!"

She tried to scramble and catch the dog, but Sheila was already in Parker's arms, wagging and yipping and licking.

Seemed to him that Parker had this under control, so he just stepped in front of Lilian when she tried to follow. "All good. He's got this."

"Who are you? You're trespassing on my land. Get off."

"He's my lover. Momma, Heath. We'll be out of your hair in a minute." Parker popped the dog in his jacket and zipped it up like it was the most natural action on earth.

"That's my dog!"

Parker didn't answer.

He hadn't seen one second of the sweet little helpless Southern lady, which was kind of amusing. "Is the camper all set, babe?"

"We're close. You back this thing up like you were born to it."

"You can't have that. I'm calling the police. You're coming in with your fuck buddy and stealing my trailer!"

Parker's response was to whistle, the sound weirdly merry.

"We're much more serious than fuck buddies. Also, I know the man who gave Parker that trailer, and I am happy to meet the sheriff and tell him as much."

"Oh, do hush. He's my son. I know him. I have a buyer for that trailer."

"Yeah?" Parker smiled. "Huh. You about ready, babe?"

She stepped up on the porch, grabbing a shotgun. "You aren't going to take that dog."

"Get in the truck, honey." Parker stood between him and his mom, advancing on her. "If you're going to shoot me, you'd better kill me with your first shot."

He froze. Walking away didn't seem like the right thing to do here. He pulled out his phone. "You're not going to shoot your own son, Lilian. You want to call the sheriff, be my guest. Or I can."

Parker stared her down, and suddenly she crumpled to the ground and began to sob, wailing, the firearm dropping to her side. Parker kicked it away, picked it up, and threw it, the shotgun going end over end.

"You ready to go?"

"I am." He took Parker's hand as they turned their back on that awful woman. "You driving, or am I?"

"I can. We'll stop and buy dog stuff when we pass a

Walmart." Parker's face was stiff, lips pursed. "She needs food and a leash."

"Mhm." He handed Parker the keys and didn't ask questions. They had days of driving to talk. "Sounds like a plan."

"Parker! You get your ass—"

Parker made it to the truck, and they slid in, the vitriol stopping as the doors closed. Once Parker closed the door, he started the truck and unzipped his coat a little, a sweet fuzzy tan face appearing.

He smiled at her. "Hey, little girl. We drove a long way to get you."

"Heath, this is Sheila. Sheila, this is Mr. Heath." Parker took a shaky breath. "Well, that was fun…"

"Oh yeah? I've never had a shotgun pointed at me before. Gotta say, though, I kind of saw it coming." He rested a hand on Parker's leg and squeezed gently. "We did it."

"We did. I want to head toward home, cool?"

Home.

He liked that.

"Cool. I'm in." He petted Sheila's fuzzy head. "I'm so in."

"Me too." A single tear clung to Parker's eyelashes as they turned back out, turning away from the long driveway.

"Hey. I love you. I'm sorry she doesn't see you the way I do."

"I—I love you too. I'm so sorry. Thank you for this. It means the world."

He could have gone his whole life without anyone pointing a gun at him, and that would have been okay. But honestly, he'd do it again in a heartbeat for Parker. "Babe, that was the hardest thing I have ever seen anyone do. It's up there with Skyler learning to walk again. Don't apologize. I had no idea it was going to be this hard on you when I suggested we do this."

"Yeah, but it's done, and we have Sheila. That's important." Parker was shivering now, and he turned up the heater.

"We do. She's adorable." He watched Parker for a little bit. "Are you sure you don't want me to drive?"

"I just want to be away from here, and then yes. I think maybe I'll need that."

"Okay, babe. Anything you need. Just breathe for now. It's over." He kept contact with a hand on Parker's leg, squeezing every so often to remind the cowboy that he was there.

"It's over. That's right. This hurts my heart, being a bad son."

"You're not a bad son!" He hadn't meant to be so strident, but Parker had it all wrong. "Those thoughts are abuse and trauma, Parker, not truth."

"Trauma? You think?" Parker's cheeks went dark red. "I mean, I'm not a victim."

"No. Not a victim. A survivor." He didn't know a lot about this, but he knew enough from his family law work to at least say something helpful.

"I guess so. I like that better." Parker gave him a wink, a weak smile.

"You don't owe her anything. She will always be your mom, and I get that it's complicated, but you're not a bad son, a bad person, or any of the things she's tried to make you believe."

"I just..." Parker stroked Sheila with one hand. "I'm glad to be coming home with you."

He nodded. "I love that you know it's your home."

"Our home?" Parker asked.

"Yeah. Ours. You and me." He grinned a little. "And that goddamn garage."

"Just think how much bigger it'll have to be now..."

He started giggling. "Well, fuck."

"Right? The world's biggest garage. A two-truck and one-trailer garage."

"Don't forget the snowmobile. Maybe we build the trailer its own cover." He snorted. They'd be building for a year.

"Oh man, our sweet baby trailer with its very own carport..." Parker was giggling now.

"Never say I don't know how to spoil you." Heath was laughing and after all that tension, it felt so good.

"Well, at least I brought a dowry, right?"

They both howled with laughter, and he felt like, finally, they were on their way.

## 19

Sheila jumped around the bed.

Jumped down.

Begged to be lifted up.

Ran around the bed.

Jumped down.

Begged to get up.

Parker couldn't stop laughing. Sweet, evil fuzzy beast.

"You know that game where you try to match a pet to the owner? I would have been able to match the two of you in a heartbeat." Heath's eyes were still closed, and he didn't even lift his head from the pillow.

Was he supposed to be offended?

He didn't think so.

He thought Sheila was doing great. She loved traveling, and she was in an amazing mood.

Heath picked his head up. "I forgot how early pups get you up. And she hasn't even had coffee."

"Nope, but she is a morning baby, isn't she?"

She pounced Heath as soon as he moved, barking happily, telling him good morning.

Heath usually woke up more slowly, but he perked right up, giving her scritches and kissing the top of her head. "Sheila baby! Good morning. Yes, it's early. Sooooo early."

Her little bark answered him like she knew just what he was saying.

Lord, he loved that sound. It was so damn good.

"She needs a walk, huh? Is it my turn?" Heath yawned and stretched up tall.

"Probably, yeah. I'm going to make a little dog run for her when we get home, and a doggie door, too." It would make life a ton easier.

"You might think twice about the doggie door in winter." Heath winked at him, already pulling on sweats.

"Do they not keep the cold out well enough?" He would figure something out.

"I don't know. I've never had one. We'll research. How does she feel about snow?" Heath had pulled on a hoodie and was stepping into sneakers.

"She loves it. I took her to Denver once, and she bounced around like a kangaroo."

Heath laughed and clipped Sheila's leash on her, which only made her more excited. "Awesome. You ready, miss? Let's go pee."

She ran around in a wild circle, and then she kept circling, all the way out of the trailer.

"Goofball," he heard Heath say as they left, then the trailer door shut behind them.

Parker looked at his phone, which had about a hundred missed calls from his family and one from Sky, so he called his friend back. "Hey, man. We're heading back home."

"No shit? How did it go?"

"She pulled a shotgun on Heath. We got the trailer and Sheila. We're well away now and not in any hurry."

"She—what? Park. What the fuck?" Sky was stuttering and sounded angry.

"It might not have been loaded." He didn't know. "I wasn't going to let her shoot him, no worries. She was unhappy."

"Parker." Sky sighed. "Never mind. You're on your way home? Where are you? You're in the trailer?"

"We're outside Tulsa. We stopped early to clean and stock the trailer, let Heath know Sheila." The trailer had been in pretty good shape, really. They'd pulled out a few bits of stale food, some frozen stuff, and Heath had insisted on new pillows and sheets and blankets, just in case.

"I can't wait to see her. We'll try to keep Bruiser from eating her as a snack."

"I'm more worried about Walter eating her, man." That cat was evil.

Sky hooted. "My Walter is not evil. He just doesn't like you. And I have never figured out why. Did you say something mean to him?"

"Never. You know I like critters."

"That must be it. You think he's a creature and not a god."

He snorted and rolled his eyes. "Listen to you. Beck doesn't think he's a god."

"No, Beck worships *me*."

"I heard that!"

"Good!"

He chuckled softly. "You're both rotten. I'm ready to come home, do...something worthwhile."

"Well, worthwhile might be a little bit of stretch for you, but we love having you around."

"Shut up. I'll go to work at the feed store or something, don't you stress it."

"I'm not stressing. I'm teasing. There's lots you can do around here, and there is no hurry."

He knew it. He'd figure it out once he was home. "I miss you guys. Tell the kids I'll bring presents."

"Will do. We miss you both. Drive safe and stay in touch."

"We will. It's going to be okay. We'll take it slow."

Heath came back in carrying Sheila. "Babe? Do you have a towel? She got into the mud."

"I do." He hopped up and grabbed one out of the little linen closet. "Here we go."

"Thanks."

"Sounds like you better run. Say hi to Heath for us! Later!" Sky hung up.

Heath wet the towel and washed Sheila's feet and belly. "She was chasing some critter."

"You are only tiny, girl baby. No chasing critters." He wrapped her in a towel, laughing as she licked his chin.

"It was a mouse, I think? But I don't think she knows how tiny she is." Heath laughed.

"She has no idea. She thinks she's a damn mountain lion or dire wolf or something. She thinks she's absolutely huge." He wasn't going to ever do anything to disabuse her of that notion either. He loved her ferocity.

"It's a nice morning. Good day for a hike. Or a scenic drive." Heath handed her off and she stuck her tongue out and licked him.

"Do you want to do that? We could totally have a wander." He loved how curious Heath was.

"Yeah?" Heath looked excited. "Not a whole day thing, but maybe a couple of hours before we get on the road? It's really beautiful out there."

"Sure, love. I'm on your schedule now, and I'd love to explore with you." He couldn't help but smile.

"Great. Breakfast and coffee first, now that Shiela is all walked. You want Cheerios? Did we buy any milk?"

"We did. There's milk and bananas both." He pulled down a couple of cereal bowls and rinsed them off, just in case.

"I'll make the coffee." Heath had taken to the trailer like he'd lived in it for years. He instinctively understood the little tango they had to do in the kitchen to get things done.

Sheila had curled up in her favorite spot on the window box and was watching them, waiting so patiently for her turn to eat.

He'd found her a rainbow bed, and a bunch of toys at the Walmart, along with a couple of sweaters, food, bowls, treats, and a new collar with purple rhinestones.

She liked purple best.

"We have to be home by the day after New Year's Day, but not before. We can take our time. Where do you want to ring in the new year, babe?"

He pondered that for a second, but literally only that long. "At home. I want to start there."

Heath's smile lit up those blue eyes. "I love that. Starting fresh for the new year. So we have a few days to wander home then."

"We do. We can do anything, see anything." He wanted to give Heath the entire world.

Heath was in front of the fridge and handed him the milk. "We'll make a plan. See something awesome to make us laugh. Make a memory. This trip started out kind of rough, but it's ours now and we can make it whatever we want."

He was damn lucky to have this man, that was for sure. "You know it. Our road trip home."

Sheila yipped, her tail wagging once.

"Yes, you too, silly girl. You're going to love your new home."

"Do you think she uh..." Heath kind of grinned and kind of winced at the same time. "Would she like living with other dogs?"

"Are you kidding? She loves other dogs. She traveled with me, so she's used to having to meet a ton of different animals—dogs, cats, bulls, horses."

"Oh. Cool." Heath relaxed. "I really want dogs."

Dogs. Plural.

Huh.

He could go there. "I love dogs. I think they make us better humans."

"I've never gotten one because I live—lived—alone and I didn't think it was fair with no one home all day most of the time, you know? But two of us could work it out."

"Absolutely. What kind of dogs do you think you'd want?" Two of us. God, he loved them.

"I don't know." Heath glanced at Sheila. "Bigger? Mutts. Shelter rescues. Must like snow."

"I love it. So long as they get along with Miss Priss over there, I'm in." She watched every move they made, and when he sat at the little table, she hopped up to see what they were doing.

"Oh, she's first. It's her house." Heath poured their coffee, then filled her bowl with kibble and joined him at the table. "I do love cereal."

"Me too, especially in the summer." He tilted his head. "What's your position on grits?"

He had an Instant Pot deal here in the trailer. He knew how to make those and...well, those.

Heath raised an eyebrow. "I have never had them. What should it be?"

"I love them. Like love them with butter, salt, pepper, and a sprinkle of cheese. Do you know about polenta?"

"I know about it. I have eaten it, and I like it, but I have no idea how you make it. I'm a good eater, but I'm a terrible cook."

"Well, grits is sort of like polenta. I make grits in the Instant Pot deal."

"I've heard of those. I don't have one, but I'm ready to try your grits. They sound good." Heath took another big bite of his cereal.

"Oh, cool." That was handy. He'd buy some to make while they were out here. It was a weird...well, he couldn't call it a skill. It was water, milk, and grits in the cooker, twelve minutes on, fifteen minutes waiting.

Not a skill.

"Beckett texted me while Sheila and I were out walking. That's why she got after the mouse. I got distracted for a second. He asked if I was okay...?"

Weird. He arched an eyebrow. "You are, right? You're glad to be heading home with me?"

"I am over the moon to be going anywhere with you, but every time you say 'home' I get goosebumps. For real. I thought maybe you told Skyler something."

Not that he knew of. "Just that we went home and Momma misbehaved."

Heath shrugged. "I told Beckett we're more than good."

"We are. We're road tripping." He stole a hot, happy kiss. "I can't think of anything more fun to do with our clothes on, love."

"Okay. Let's do this hike. I just need my boots. Should we pack some snacks?" Sheila hopped up like she knew something fun was about to happen. "Oops. I said S-N-A-C-K-S."

Sheila sniffed at Heath's fingers. She wasn't fooled.

"We should. I'll get her backpack. She'll get tired." He opened the closet, her backpack right there.

"I bet. I think she takes like four steps for every one of mine." Heath found his boots and traded them for his sneakers. "We bought some granola bars, right?"

"Maybe forty and yeah, there are...you want soft or crunchy. We bought both." They were great at snacks.

"Crunchy, for sure. This is going to sound ridiculous, but I always thought I would end up with someone who could cook, and I am so glad I didn't." Heath grinned. "That's too much pressure."

Parker cackled. "Shit, you and me? We got Sky and Beck, frozen pizza, and mac and cheese in a box. Life is good."

They were also super capable of ordering out.

"So good." Heath helped him pack the granola bars. "You about ready to get out there?"

"Let's hit it." He was in, all the way. "C'mon, baby girl. Let's go." He had her a coat, booties, a little collapsable water dish.

He was ready.

## 20

The trail they chose led to a tree-lined clearing with a stream, some picnic tables, and a grassy area that Heath could tell Sheila was itching to run around in. She'd been a trouper, but she'd given up trotting along with them and had ended up in her little backpack long ago.

"Hey, this is pretty." Heath dropped his own backpack on one of the tables.

"It is. It's chilly, but not bitter cold. I like it." Parker sat on the edge of the picnic table, glancing around. "It's not as pretty as home, but it's nice."

"The sun is nice." Heath took Sheila out of the backpack and strapped on her leash. "Let's run, girl."

"Oh my God. Aren't you cute with her?" Parker beamed at them and hopped down.

He grinned at Parker and took off for the clearing at a brisk walk, Sheila trotting along with him. "Run, run, run!" He laughed, watching Sheila's little legs go a mile a minute.

Parker was cackling, his joy ringing out.

This had been the right idea. The worried lines around Parker's mouth had eased.

He hadn't ever seen anything like what happened at Parker's mother's house. He'd never met anyone like that woman. That much hatred for someone she gave birth to was impossible for him to understand.

Especially talking about Parker, who was maybe the kindest person he'd ever been involved with. Parker made him smile without trying.

Parker knocked their shoulders together. "I hate being somewhere I can't kiss you."

Heath gave him a confused look and wandered back toward him. "Why can't you kiss me? You won't embarrass Sheila; she watched us fuck last night."

"This isn't a safe place, love. We're not in gay-friendly territory."

He hated that they had to consider things like that everywhere they went. He looked around and stepped in close to Parker. "There's no one here but us, babe."

"In that case." Parker kissed him, the act soft and so sweet.

"Mm." If it wasn't so chilly he'd like to lay out a blanket in the grass and soak up some sun with his man. "See? We survived."

"We did. I...thank you, huh? Seriously."

He nodded. "We had to get out of our heads, you know? Breathe some good air. See some good sky."

"Yes. I needed to...restart."

"That's what we're doing. That's what this whole trip is about. Restarting together. You, me and Sheila. We're going home where people love you." He grinned. "With added snow."

"Bonus snow! My favorite!" Parker cackled, rolled his eyes. "So much more fun than making giant mudmen..."

"Oh, mudmen. Sounds like a blast." He took a quick kiss,

and Sheila started nipping at his heels. "Oh, she's feeling left out."

Parker scooped her up, nuzzling her as she wagged furiously, her entire backside wiggling.

He walked along the little brook that went through the area and crouched to feel the water. "Cold. Wow."

"Yeah, it may not snow much, but that water's got to be bitter."

"Clear though. Nice."

"There are decent things about this part of the country. It's easy to demonize it."

He wandered back to Parker, feeling free and daring. "I think I want to blow you up here. Pick a tree to duck behind."

"What?" Parker shook his head, looking around. "No, lover, we can't. We can get arrested or worse. Come to the trailer, and we can do it, but it's not safe."

"No? I'm a lawyer." He winked. "There is no one here, babe. No one."

"You're my lawyer-jack." Parker took his hand, squeezed it. "And I need to protect you."

"We need to be back in Vermont. When no one is around up there, no one is going to be around." He snorted. "Raincheck then."

"We do." Parker smiled at him, the expression wry. "This isn't a friendly place, lover. I wish it was, but wishing doesn't make it so."

"It's as beautiful as it is disappointing." He rolled his eyes. "Granola bar?"

"Please. At least I'm not disappointing, right?"

"Never. Not one time since I met you." He handed one over and got one out for himself, and a treat for Sheila.

"Thanks. I can't imagine being disappointed in you."

"Oh, I'm sure I'll figure out some way eventually." He grinned and took a big bite of his granola bar.

"No, I don't think so. I think that we're okay." Parker looked down and looked up again, stopping, kind of waving his granola bar around. "I know it hasn't been very long. I know that. But it doesn't matter. I don't care. You're my person, and I'm gonna do right by you."

Heath took a deep breath and nodded. That should probably scare him, but it didn't. He probably should be getting slow-down vibes, but he wasn't getting those either. "I'm going to take care of you, Parker. Like the precious, amazing, beautiful person you are. I know how lucky I am."

Parker took his hand and squeezed it. "Know that our first New Year's Eve isn't going to be our last. I'm a cowboy. I'm a loyal man. And when I say in twenty years we'll be having our twentieth Happy New Year kiss, I mean it."

He stared into Parker's eyes, feeling breathless, feeling like his heart was going to beat right out of chest. Or shake him to bits. Or just explode. There was really only one thing to say to that.

"Okay. I do."

## 21

God, Parker loved the zoo.

Miss Sheila was at a Doggy Daycare, safe and sound, and they were spending the day taking pictures of bears playing in the snow, orangutans swinging like they weighed nothing, and rhinos that didn't have to do anything but stand there and be amazing.

He was having a ball, and Heath?

Heath was magical.

"In my next life, I'm coming back as an elephant."

"Ooh...would you do sexy things with your...trunk?" He couldn't stop his chuckle.

"Dork. I suppose I could. I was thinking more about being so majestic and deliberate. Commanding respect."

"You're pretty deliberate, honey." And he knew folks respected Heath. He had no question.

Heath snorted, grinning. "Okay, maybe. But I'm not majestic. I could come back as a lemur instead. Live the good life."

"Oh, I like that. I think I'd want to be a bird." Flying sounded wicked cool.

"And fly? Yeah, that would be neat. You'd be a pretty bird."

"Unless I got reborn as an emu. Or an albatross..."

"Then you'd be big and ugly. But I'd still love you." Heath's head tilted. "Can emus fly?"

"Nope. They can't. But they do drop their feathers in a wad when they're scared."

Heath barked out a laugh loud enough he actually had to apologize to the people standing near them. "That just seems so...not you."

"Yeah, I'm not likely to drop trou in fear, but..." He started laughing too, tickled shitless.

"Not in fear." Heath was still giggling. "We're going to cause a scene."

"Only if we're nasty, right? We're not going to be gross."

Heath rolled his eyes at him. "No, babe. We are never gross. I'm just playing with you."

"Me too." He winked at Heath. "Although, I could so be gross with you."

"Speaking of gross, are there penguins? I want to see penguins."

"There have to be penguins. They don't make penguin-free zoos. Penguins are numerous, and they can't escape." Right?

"Cool. Let's find them." Heath took a couple of steps, then looked over at him. "So is this a no-holding-hands zone too, or am I allowed a little PDA?"

"I've never been here, but Indianapolis is supposed to be a friendly city, huh?" Parker took Heath's hand.

Heath's smile grew wide and his shoulders squared up. "Good. This is great."

Parker examined their map. "Yep. You want to get lunch

on the way to the penguins? We're on the other side of the zoo from them."

"Can I get a zoo-dog? You know, a foot-long hot dog. And fries." Heath stroked a thumb over his hand.

"Ooh... Hell, yes. I want a smash burger and fries. Do you want ranch or ketchup on your fries?"

"Ranch is weird, so ketchup." Heath grinned at him. "I mean, ranch is fine for some people...or uh... ranch is... I mean, to each his own."

Parker snorted softly. Teasing Heath was more fun than color TV. "Ranch dressing is amazing, and you know I love it. Pizza. Fries. Jalapeno poppers. Onion rings. Yum!"

"See? Weird." Heath pulled him over to a cafeteria-style food court, and they loaded up a tray with greasy zoo food. "So," Heath said as they sat down. "I want a garage and a deck off the bedroom. What do you want?"

Parker pursed his lips, tilted his head. "Let's make a game slash media room. Somewhere we can hang out and have fun together."

"Finish the basement, or add a room over the garage, maybe. Add a Ping Pong table and some comfy recliners." Heath nodded. "I like it."

"Yeah. We need a space that's just ours, right?"

"The whole place will feel like ours soon I hope."

"Well, I hope I can help you a lot—in all the ways."

"So far so good." Heath took a huge bite of his hot dog. "Oh, so bad it's good."

"I love a hot dog, man, especially in the summer on the grill. That and beer can chicken."

Heath grinned. "Is that when you stand the whole chicken on a beer can and cook it?"

"Yep. You shove a beer can up a chicken's butt and cook that critter."

"Sounds great. We'll do it for Skyler and Beckett this summer. I'm way better on the grill than I am in the kitchen."

"You and me both, honey. You and me both." He noshed on his burger, so damn happy.

"I'm going to have to go back to work when we get home. What's your plan do you think? Job? Sleep all day? Find three more dogs?"

"Oh, I'm going to work. I can do construction, or if there's someone who needs handyman work. Hell, if there's a hardware store, I'll get something there. I'm not proud." And he had some cushion too.

"You would look hot in a hard hat." Heath winked at him. "What about horses? Do you like horses? My neighbor, Jake's son Tim runs some kind of breeding or training thing on Jake's land. Not sure what he does exactly, but Jake is always telling me how busy Tim is. I was going ask if Tim needed anyone..."

"I can totally work horses. I grew up with them and have worked with them my entire career."

Heath nodded. "I'll introduce you to Tim."

Parker smiled at him. He wasn't too proud. He knew he needed to network.

Heath reached over and stole his pickle, taking a big bite of it with a grin.

"Oh, my poor pickle!" He clasped his hands over his chest, going for totally dramatic.

"Mhm. Murdered. RIP. It was delicious." Heath pushed over the plate of fries as compensation.

"Thanks, love." He took a perfectly crispy fry—one of the fries that were almost translucent with the crunch.

"I can't remember the last time I was at a zoo. I think I was a kid. Like, six or eight. It was in Buffalo. We don't really have zoos in Vermont. There's a neat reindeer farm though in Orleans and a few wildlife conservation areas."

"Oh, can we go? I want to see reindeers. Are they friendly?" He wanted to pet their antlers.

"Oh yeah, we can go. You want to?" Heath's eyes lit up. "Some of them are friendly, they have feed and stuff. It's fun."

"I'd love it. Any time." He was a goof for that sort of shit.

"Good. We'll go while it's still winter. They're pretty in the snow." Heath stuffed the last bite of hot dog into his mouth.

He waited until Heath swallowed to drawl, "You eat that sausage awful pretty..."

Heath flushed pink and snorted out a laugh. "You—you don't say?"

"I do." He waggled his eyebrows, playing along madly. "I really, really do."

"Evil. So evil." Heath picked up his Coke and took a long sip.

"Mmhmm." Evil, but fun? He was loads of fun, and Heath liked it, he could tell.

"Finish your burger, evil man. I want to go see the smelly penguins." Heath looked down into his own lap, then back up again and winked. "I think I'm presentable."

"You are free of traces of ketchup and or mustard. I can be seen with you."

"I was more concerned about whether I should come out from behind this table..."

"Oh." He loved that. It genuinely made him feel ten thousand feet tall.

"Oh, you say?" Heath laughed. "You and your evil sausage comment had me all heated up for a minute."

"Hey. I'm the one who has to watch your gorgeous

mouth all the time." It was a wonder he didn't have blue balls.

Heath licked his lips and winked. "I'm so sorry for you."

"I know." He put his hand on his heart, so dramatic. "I'm so brave."

"Pfft. Okay. Let's go, Lancelot." Heath stood. "Penguins."

"Penguins, ho!" He laughed—how he could go from miserable to happy to miserable to happy so fast? He had no idea.

---

The zoo had been a brilliant idea, if Heath did say so himself. So far, Operation Keep Parker Distracted was working like a charm. Once they were home, it wouldn't take so much thought, but this trip had a shadow over it, and he was determined to lift it and keep it there.

He had another plan hatching too. It involved buying a ring and talking to his mom. And possibly a dog-sitter, if Parker would be okay with that.

But that was still in the early stages, and he couldn't let himself get distracted right now.

He knew they were close to the penguin enclosure by the smell. He loved those slimy, slippery, waddling creatures, but, man—they smelled like death.

Parker kept beaming at him, eyes on him like Parker couldn't not look, and it made Heath feel a thousand feet tall.

He kept hold of Parker's hand because Parker had said it was okay. He didn't want to let go. He wanted everyone who saw them to know that this gorgeous, kind, sweet gentleman was his.

"There they are!" He tugged Parker along, excited to see

his favorite creature in the zoo. Tigers were cool. Elephants were astounding, but penguins were funny as hell and he loved them.

"I love how they look so clumsy on land and so damn stunning in the water. It's magic."

"Right? And I'm sure they're fishing or something, but they always look like they're playing to me. Just having fun."

"Did you know they have solid bones?" Parker was reading the plaques on the wall, fascinated.

"Nope. They seem like pretty squishy." He was watching them dive and swim and climb out of the water. "I love how they just kind of pop up. Doesn't seem like it should work, you know?"

"Also, they got no teeth. They have sharp ridge-y things to hold the fish." Parker leaned in, dropped his voice to a bare whisper. "No BJs for them."

"Aw! So sad to be a penguin." He laughed. "Have you ever looked in their mouths though? It's terrifying. Seriously."

"I hadn't, no. That's so wild, man. Nature is amazing."

He lowered his voice as well. "We can make up for all of their lost BJ opportunities." They could start as soon as they got back to the trailer.

"Oh, I love how you think, Penguin Man."

"Yeah, well. Make sure you thank the right head." He couldn't stop his laugh.

"I so will." Parker goosed him, so careful no kids would see it.

"Parker!" he hissed and rolled his eyes. "Not in front of the penguins."

"Oh, right. We can't tease. They can't blow or pinch..."

He tilted his head thoughtfully. "I bet they can spank

with their little flippers." He made a spanking-flipper gesture and cracked himself up.

Parker snorted, the laughter barely held in. "You got to think that mating is...awkward with those guys."

"At least." He had no idea how that worked. He could look it up, but he liked the mystery of it. "They're so loud. They might have you beat."

"Hey, I spent a lifetime being quiet, you know. You make it impossible."

"Yeah?" That made him feel like a giant. "Well, keep it up. Shout all you like, I love it."

"I intend to, and I love you too." Parker gave him a warm glance.

"Excuse me?" A teenager holding hands with a girl who was obviously his girlfriend walked right up to Parker. "Mr. Stephens? You're Parker Stephens."

"I am." Suddenly Parker seemed to light up, expression turning to something Heath didn't quite recognize as he held out his hand. "Pleased to meet you."

"Good to meet you too, sir. I'm Louis, this is Amy. Wow. At the zoo. So cool." The kid patted his jeans and came up with a zoo map. "Will you please sign this for me?"

"Of course. You got a pen on you?"

The kid nodded, and Parker scribbled his well-wishes on the map.

Louis squinted at Heath. "Are you famous?"

He blinked for a second, then grinned. "Totally. I am Heath, the Vermont lumberjack."

"Oh cool. The beard is awesome." The kid handed him the map to sign.

Parker nodded, playing along like it was nothing. "Isn't it? I think it's wild. I'm considering growing one myself."

He signed the map and handed it back. "I'm really nobody compared to Mr. Stephens, though. Enjoy the zoo."

Louis nodded, like he was going to leave, but paused and looked at Parker. "See you in the arena?"

Parker smiled, winked at the kid. "Never say never, right? Have a great day."

"You too, sir. Thank you. Thanks!" The kids hurried off, glancing back over their shoulders.

Parker grinned at him. "My famous lawyer-jack."

He straightened up. "That's me!" He took Parker's hand. "Never say never, huh?"

"I'm going to announce my retirement, but not to a teenager in the zoo."

"No? You don't think he'd keep it to himself? What about the penguins? You could start with them. They won't tell."

Parker lifted an eyebrow, then dragged him over to the window. "Penguins. Guys. I'm retired from bull riding."

He shook his head. "See? They give no shits."

"Do they speak English, do you think?" Parker winked at him.

"Possibly not." He chuckled. "They were a good test run."

"Let me tell you, then." Parker met his eyes. "I'm retiring from bull riding, lover."

He held that gaze and nodded. "I get you all to myself now."

"Yep. I hope you don't regret it. I intend to make sure you don't."

"Never. Not possible. Are you kidding? I got a cowboy! That's the dream, right?"

"You know it. I'm a goddamn archetype."

"Cowboy and lawyer-jack. We're a regular Sunday movie."

"Maybe a regular NC-17 movie on a Saturday night?"

"Oh we are *way* more regular than just Saturday night." He chuckled. "What else do you want to see? Or should we go check on our own beast?"

"This is the pinnacle, man—tuxedo birds of non-fellatio joy."

"Non—" He just cracked up, laughing as he gave Parker a little shove. "I guess we're done here!"

"Let's go hit the Walmart for some cards and some tater tots and chicken strips, then we'll get our girl."

Sounded perfect. "Can we get beer too? And cheese?"

"Ooh. Sharp cheddar and something weird?"

"Yeah. Exactly that. We are so good."

Parker met his eyes, took his hand and squeezed. "You know it, honey."

## 22

B y the time they pulled up to the house, the trailer was full of goodies for the children and Sky and Beck, plus neat items for Heath's work.

Parker was ready to be home, though. They'd need to winterize the trailer, unpack it.

Make a fire.

Get Sheila introduced to her new home.

Everything.

Parker blinked as he pulled in. "Where should I park the trailer, love?"

"Oh. Uh... I guess alongside the house where the garage will go?" Heath pointed. "Over there. You need me to back you in?"

He pondered that. He'd done it a thousand times, but he was tired, and it was getting dark. "You mind?"

Plus, the snow might make things tricky.

"Nope. Team, effort." Heath gave him a tired grin and hopped out of the truck.

That was them—team and effort. Parker sat there for a second, listening to Sheila wag.

"We're home, baby girl."

Heath climbed up on a snowbank and waved him back. "Okay, go for it!"

They managed together to get the trailer parked, and then he grabbed Sheila's leash and handed her out to Heath. "She loves snow."

"Okay then." Heath put her down on the path someone had dug to the front door. Not them, but someone. They hadn't been home. "Let's get you inside so we can unpack, baby girl."

"I'll start unloading. You want me coming straight into the mudroom?" They were so damn domestic.

"Sure, that sounds good. I'll clean her up, then kick my shoes off and grab stuff from you." Heath followed Sheila toward the house. "Just shout if you need a hand."

"Will do." He unhooked the truck, then started with the perishables, unloading the food.

"The house is cold. I started a fire and turned up the heat. Sheila is sacked out on the couch under a blanket." Heath took a tote full of food from him.

"Oh, cool. She isn't freaking? That's my girl. God, it's good to be home." He headed back out into the snow.

Heath was at the trailer door when he was ready to bring over the next load. "I got this one."

"Yeah?" He appreciated it, because he was starting to shiver, the cold creeping in on him.

"Sure, my turn." Heath smiled at him, no mention of the cold. "You should go check on Sheila."

"I should. I need to start laundry too, I bet." He grabbed a bunch of bags and hurried to the house.

Sheila was snoring, tail wagging under blanket, not even caring as he threw in a load of laundry before heading back out.

There was a stack of things inside the mudroom, and Heath was trudging toward the house with a suitcase and a backpack. "I think that's everything? You might want to double-check."

"I'll check, but I think anything not in here can wait overnight." He closed the door behind Heath and locked it.

"Cool. It's dark and cold. I'd rather be in here with you." Heath's cheeks were pink from the chilly air.

"With you are my two favorite words." He took the food from Heath's hands and took it to the kitchen.

Heath followed. "It's warmed up here. Sheila is good?"

"Snoring like a Latvian chainsaw drill team." Parker winked over, then stole a kiss. "Hey, you. We're home."

"We are. That was a long day, but I'm glad we pushed through."

"Me too. That gives us a chance to relax, chill out." And get ready for Heath to get back to work, and for him to get to work finding a job.

"Home in time to start the new year here." Heath smiled and took a kiss too.

"Yes. To start out like we can hold out, right?"

"You know it." Heath helped him unpack. "We have an invite to Beckett and Skyler's tomorrow night for the ball drop."

"Yeah? Do you want to go?" He was easy. They could go and stay, go early and leave early. He just didn't want to drive after midnight with the amateurs. "We can take the pupper and just spend the night, if we get toasty."

"I think we should go. I don't know about spending the night. I kind of want to wake up here, you know?" Heath glanced at him. "Make love in our own bed New Year's morning."

"Ooh... I'm in. Then let's go early, celebrate with the

family, and be home before midnight. We can watch the ball together."

"Yeah. Perfect." Heath nodded enthusiastically. "We'll say goodbye to this year and hello to the next one together."

"Excellent." He loved this plan. He wanted to ring in the New Year at home.

At their home.

"How does Sheila feel about noisemakers?"

That wasn't going to be an issue. "She's a rodeo dog. She'll be fine as frog hair."

Heath nodded. "No fireworks out here, but I do like those stupid noisemakers."

"We'll stop and grab some. Do we need to bring food or beer?" They had a lot of cheese...

"What a question." Heath laughed. "Need to, no, but should we?"

"I guess we prob'ly ought." He wrapped one arm around Heath. "We got plenty."

"Plenty of laundry." Heath winked at him.

"Tons. But I'm on it. Soon I will have clean unders for us both."

"We also have to figure out where to put all of Sheila's things. Food bowls and her bed and stuff."

"Yeah. I'm going to build her a wee dog run off the back porch. She'll like that."

"That's a great idea. I like it better than a fence." Heath caught him around the waist. "I enjoyed the trailer. It was fun."

"We can go out in it whenever. You saw how easy it was to hookup."

And leave with.

"We should plan a trip for the spring. Maybe go north to Canada. I could probably work from the road some even."

"Whatever you want. I'm a go-baby. You know that."
They settled together on the sofa, leaning together.

"You should know that I have enough to cover us. I'm not saying you should sit around here and learn to cook or anything, but..." Heath winked at him. "But you should do something you love and not worry about the dollar signs."

"I've got investments, savings. I'll be okay. I can work like a dog, for a good reason." Parker thought Heath was the best reason.

"If you want to, but you don't have to. You're not an "I" anymore, you're a "we." And we're fine."

"We are. We're better than fine."

They were home.

## 23

"Happy new year!" Charlie answered the door wearing big plastic sparkly glasses and a cardboard top hat covered in purple glitter.

"Happy new year!" Heath smiled at her. "You look so festive."

"Papa says it's never too early to celebrate." She stepped back and held the door open.

"He's right."

"Uncle Parker." Charlie's eyes lit up. "You have a tiny dog."

"This is my Sheila. Don't let Walter eat her, okay? It's important."

"He won't. Walter likes dogs."

He snorted. "You know Walter likes everyone but you, babe."

Charlie closed the door behind them, nodding sagely. "Papa says that's because Walter was stressed and lonely, and it was a scary time, and that Uncle Parker did his best."

Parker's smile was warm, and he opened his arms to Charlie. "God, I missed you, little girl."

Charlie hugged him back tight.

"Uncle Parker always does his best." Heath gave Parker a pat on the shoulder and made his way into the house.

"Heath! You're back in one piece." That was Beck's voice coming from the kitchen.

"Never had a doubt." Well, for a brief moment while staring down the barrel of a shotgun he might have worried a bit, but they handled it. He was pretty sure that between them, he and Parker could handle anything.

Not that he ever wanted to handle *that* again.

"What do you think of the trailer?"

"Oh, it's great. We're already talking about a spring trip somewhere."

"Oh? That should be fun. Where are y'all thinking?" Sky took the beer and cheese from him.

"I suggested Canada. Parker called himself a 'go-baby' and said he'd go anywhere." He wanted to talk to Sky, but he needed to get the cowboy alone somewhere. Or at least out of earshot of Parker.

"Rock on, and Happy New Year, by the way. Parker said y'all had a decent trip."

"We did. It was stressful sometimes on the way there and it was definitely rough with his mother, but it got better and better as we put some miles behind us. We're closer. It was worth it." So worth it. Parker was so damn happy and he loved that.

"I'm tickled. She was toxic. He deserves better."

He lowered his voice. "She's insane, Sky. I feel terrible for him. But I'm going to be his family now, and I'm making sure he knows that."

"That's what matters. Just be there. This hurts, but he'll get lighter every day as the infection eases."

He knew that was true, he'd seen it already. "We have plans, we have... I need to talk to you. Just you. Later?"

Sky tilted his head. "Sure. Come on back to the deck whenever, and I'll follow. Show you my Christmas smoker."

"You got a smoker?" No time like the present. He still had his coat on. "Let's go."

Sky gave him a nod and they stepped out back. He definitely had deck envy, but he knew he and Parker were going to make their house amazing. "So, what's up?"

He took a breath and blew it out. He didn't know whether he was being stupid or smart to ask this question, but he needed an answer. "How long do you have to be with someone before you propose? Is there like, a formula? Or a rule or something? Because we're making plans like it's going to happen, and I know what I want, and I just really don't want fuck it up, you know? I can't fuck this up."

"Oh." Sky stopped for a second, then grinned at him. "As far as I know, everyone makes their own rules, and Parker? Well, I don't think you can fuck this up. He's yours, balls to bones."

Heath felt his cheeks heat. "I think so too."

"Well, then. When you feel it, do it. Life moves fast, and you don't know whether you have years to think."

From anyone else that could have been a cliché, but Skyler understood better than most what an uncertain tomorrow was. He nodded. "I'm not going to let much grass grow." He knew where Beckett had gotten Skyler's ring, and he was going to make an appointment tomorrow.

"Well, we'll be tickled as shit to have you both happy and together and home." Skyler grinned at him. "And once he's settled, I'm going to talk to him about a business idea I had."

"Oh yeah? He would love that. He's so worried about

getting a job and being useful." He wanted Parker to be happy here.

"Yeah, I figured. I get it. I worried too, but I have ideas."

He nodded. "Cool. Thank you so much. Let's get you back inside, it's cold out here." He opened the slider to let Skyler go in first.

"There you are." Beckett went right to Skyler and pulled him into a hug. "You're so cold."

He shrugged apologetically. "He wanted to show me his smoker."

"Happy Christmas to him—he's spoiled rotten." Beckett winked at him. "But the turkey breast he made the other day was amazing."

"Spoiled, maybe. Rotten, never." Skyler kissed Beckett's chin.

"Parker is in the other room keeping an eye on Sheila."

*Uh-oh.* "Everything okay?"

"Oh yeah. But Walter took a shine to her, so..." Beckett gave him a lopsided grin.

He laughed. "Is Parker jealous?"

Beckett shrugged. "Maybe?"

"It could happen. Walter has been known to be a seductive little bastard."

He laughed. "Parker," he called. "Babe. Walter isn't going to eat Sheila. Come have a beer."

Noah came in, his eyes lit up. "Uncle Parker has a teeny tiny puppy! She has a diamond necklace, Pappy!"

Parker followed behind, a vaguely worried expression on his face. "You sure that demon cat won't eat my baby?"

Beckett chuckled, bending to grin at Noah. "She is the cutest, isn't she?"

"Have a beer, Park. It's not like Walter's making friends just to mess with you." Skyler handed a bottle to Parker.

"Could happen." He took Parker's hand and tugged him closer. "But I doubt it."

Charlie laughed as Bruiser pushed past her to investigate the new dog. "We're a family, Uncle Parker. Don't worry. We're going to take good care of her."

"See? Family." He couldn't help himself, and gave Parker a quick kiss, careful to keep it family-friendly too.

Parker leaned in, nodded. "So, how's the week of break been?"

Sky rolled his eyes. "Thank God for Beck's folks. They took the kids for two days so we could breathe without having any crises."

"We slept the whole first day." Beckett snorted.

He nodded. "Uh-huh. Slept. Sure."

"Okay, we stayed in bed the whole day."

Parker chuckled softly. "That's fair enough, I guess." Then he dropped his voice. "Pervs."

He started with the giggles, but he already knew he was a goner.

"Pfft." Beckett laughed. "Yeah, like the trailer wasn't rocking and rolling all the way home from Oklahoma."

"Did you play music in the trailer, Uncle Parker?" Noah asked, and he'd be damned if Parker didn't just nod and keep a straight face.

"We did. We sang a lot."

"A lot." He couldn't hold back his laughter.

"Uncle Heath's throat was hoarse from singing."

He lost it, doubling over. God, he couldn't breathe.

Everyone was laughing along—even though the other two couldn't possibly know what they were laughing at.

"Oh, God. You guys broke Uncle Heath." Charlie gave him a little push, and he just collapsed to the ground giggling.

"Get him, Sierra. Tickle him." Parker was not helping, and Beckett's youngest tackle hugged him, wiggling, little fingers digging into his ribs.

He was starting to get it together, but Sierra was the cutest kid on earth, so he played along. "Oh no. No tickling. Mercy! Mercy!"

"Mercy!" She giggled and kissed his cheek. "Happy year!"

"Oh. Thank you." He sighed and went limp when she stopped tickling. "Happy year to you too, sweetheart."

Charlie groaned. "It's happy *new* year, dodohead."

"Happy year!" Sierra repeated.

"Ugh." Charlie rolled her eyes. "Hopeless."

Sky winked at Parker. "She was never hopeless. Ever."

"Nope. Not once." Parker grabbed Sierra, swinging her around. "Happy Year, ladybug."

She giggled happily. "Happy year, Uncle Park!"

He hauled himself off the floor and picked up his beer. "Whoo. My sides hurt."

"How long until New Year, Pappy?"

"Longer than your bedtime, partner." Beckett gave Noah a bowl of popcorn.

"Aw. No fair."

"Hm. What's not fair is you being tired all day and me being grumpy. Plus, school starts on the second."

"School!" Sierra seemed pleased by that.

Charlie was not. "Ugh."

Noah jumped up and wiggled his butt. "I love school."

"Not me. I hate school. I want to be a cowboy like my Papa."

Beckett glanced at Skyler and shook his head but didn't say a thing. Which, he thought said more than words.

Tweens were tough. Keira said so all the time.

"Uh...should we put the cheese out?"

"Hooray cheese!" Noah ran up to him. "Can I help?"

"Yep. Come on, kiddo." He led Noah to the kitchen.

Parker followed right behind, hand on his waistband. "I'm right behind you to get the cheese."

He tucked a hand behind him to take Parker's. "You're so good with these kids."

"I love them. They're part of our family." Parker beamed at him, and Heath loved how his lover was visibly relaxing.

"Mhm. They are." He poked around and found a cutting board that would work for the cheese. As much as he wanted Parker to himself tonight, they'd made the right choice to come here for a while.

"You want to cut some up too?" Parker found a butter knife and one of the softer cheeses, and little Noah beamed at him.

"I do! I can help, Uncle. I'm a good helper."

"Of course you are, kiddo."

"So, are you the parent type or the rile up the kids and send them back to their own parents type?" He'd meant that as a conversational question but quickly realized that asking Parker probably made it a bigger one than he'd meant it to be.

Parker glanced over. "Is that your way of asking if I want to be a daddy one day?"

He felt his cheeks warm up. "Well, accidentally, but since I asked, do you?"

"Yeah. I mean, if not, I'll live, but yeah. I would like to follow Sky's example and show the world another good father."

He smiled, lifting Noah up to sit on a stool. "Or two. I've never given it thought because I just assumed—I mean, you know." He'd just assumed it wasn't a thing. He was single, he was getting older.

"I do, but we were wrong." Parker grinned at him. "Because we are."

He nodded thoughtfully. "Yeah. Here we are."

Noah pretended to cut on the counter with the butter knife. "I like cheese."

"Me too! Here buddy, cut this one." Parker immediately handed Noah a piece of softer cheese.

So that was their future. A ring, kids, a garage and a second-story deck with an incredible view.

Exploring in the trailer.

And dogs.

Which reminded him, "Hey, Skyler said he needs to talk to you about a business thing."

"Yeah?" Parker didn't seem worried. "Cool. I'll talk to him after the holidays. He's always planning something."

"Maybe this something will be a good opportunity for you." He hoped so, he wanted Parker to like it here—to be busy and useful and happy.

"If it isn't, something will come up. Something always does." Parker stole a kiss.

"You definitely make your own luck." He loved that about Parker. But from here on out, he was going to make sure Parker didn't need luck. Starting at midnight, they were going to make plans instead.

---

PARKER WALKED Sheila before heading in for their evening, their midnight bubbly waiting for them. The house looked amazing. The tree was lit up still, the snow was falling.

It was beautiful.

He could see Heath through the kitchen window; he was dancing around wearing the gold sparkly tiara that Sierra had put on him and opening and closing cabinets, looking for something.

"God, I love him," he whispered. "Thank you—whoever you are—for bringing us together."

Heath pumped a fist in the air and pulled two champagne glasses out of a cabinet.

He chuckled and shook his head and headed inside to celebrate. "Hey, you. It looks beautiful from out there."

"The tree or the house? I found the champagne glasses!" Heath brandished them like trophies.

"Oh, nice. The tree in the house." He unhooked Sheila and let her go, her little paws tip-tapping through the house.

Heath tucked an arm around him. "Oh, babe. You're cold. The fire's going. Do you want me to open the champagne?"

"Are we close to the time?" He slipped one hand around Heath's waist. "Or do you want bubbly first and midnight hanky-panky?"

"Pfft. I always want hanky-panky. Is that even a question?"

"Oh, then pop the cork, honey. I want to suck you with bubbles on my tongue."

"Woohoo!" Heath lit up brighter than fireworks and went after the bottle. "I'm on it!"

He chuckled and went to take off his boots and slide into the fuzzy slippers they'd found him. "I'm glad we decided to come home early."

"Me too. There's something right about wrapping up this year and starting the next one together." Heath wrapped a towel around the bubbly and tugged on the cork.

He grinned, impressed. He didn't know that he'd ever opened a bottle of champagne. Hopefully he liked it.

The pop was impressive, and Heath poured two glasses, then looked at his watch. "Almost time."

"Come to the bedroom?" They could ring in the year there, bare butt naked and happy.

"Lead the way, babe." Heath put a hand on his back and followed him, turning off lights as they went. "I don't ever drink champagne except on New Year's Eve."

"I've never tried before, but people talk about the bubbles." And he liked beer bubbles.

"It's very bubbly." Heath set his glass down on the dresser and tugged off his sweater. "Naked new year?"

"You know it. My favorite thing—naked new year for us."

"Best New Year's ever!" Heath started stripping, clothes landing in a pile on the floor.

"Yet. Best New Year's yet." He got naked, cock filling.

"First best New Year's ever?" Heath winked at him and slid a hand down his chest.

"Uh-huh." His eyelids got heavy, his tongue slipping out to wet his lips.

Heath leaned in close and whispered. "Hold that thought, I need to turn on the TV." Heath was giggling as he picked up the remote.

"Uh-huh. You'll have to count down." He sipped the champagne, the bubbles tickling his nose.

"Mhm. Just a couple of minutes until bubbly BJ time." Heath turned on New Year's Rockin' Eve.

Parker grinned at Heath, and pulled his man close, only keeping track of the noise on the TV with half an ear.

Last year he'd been sitting outside in Oklahoma, drinking a beer and watching the stars.

Heath kissed him gently. "We're going to have a great year. I know it."

"Why wouldn't we? It's a new beginning for us. New work. New building. You have a dog and a cowboy of your own."

"I do. And he's naked too." Heath glanced at the TV. "Oh. Glasses. One minute to midnight."

"You have a wish, lover?" He did. He wished they would be here, together, next year.

"I don't know." Heath looked right into his eyes. "You might have made them all come true already."

All he could do was push into a kiss, letting Heath know how much Parker loved him.

It didn't matter if they missed midnight, his bell was ringing.

They heard it though, the crowd, the cheering, and Heath pulled back just enough to whisper, "Three. Two. One."

He took a deep drink of champagne and swooped down, lips wrapping around Heath's cock.

Happy fucking New Year.

# EPILOGUE

Heath really wanted to try it himself, but dealing with concrete during mud season was best left to the professionals. They'd had a huge slab poured, big enough for the two-car garage, a covered port for the trailer and a workshop that connected the house to the garage and kept the thing from looking as monstrous as it was.

The footprint was nearly as big as the house itself, but it was going to be great. Their trucks would be tucked away from the snow leaving a big open, clear driveway for the plow—and the workshop was a smart addition. They'd even put in a potbelly stove. That was Parker's idea, so they could still do some DIY in the wintertime.

The walls went up quickly and they were roofing now. It was perfect timing, because they'd have it done before summer warmed everything up. Heath dug around for some nails, or pretended to. He was actually taking a second to watch Parker hammer away in the sunshine. So sexy. So capable.

Parker had been having a ball working with Sky, helping to create a series of small bull riding events all over the northeast, but his cowboy still had plenty of time to help with the construction and spend time with him, so it was a win-win.

He squinted at the sky. It was late afternoon, there was a storm in the forecast, and he'd rather be grilling and drinking a beer.

"Hey, babe? You want to wrap it up and call it day?"

"You know it. It's hot, and it's fixin' to pour down." Parker shot him a happy grin.

"I was thinking burgers. You in?" He started cleaning up, putting tools into a bucket and lowering them down on a rope.

"Perfect. We got chips and onion dip. Nom nom nom."

The barking from the dog run started as soon as they stepped off the ladder.

"Hello, ladies! Have you missed us?"

Sheila jumped up and down with her little doggie smile and Waffle, their new little terrier and *something* mix-breed rescue was running back and forth behind her, wiry fur flopping in her eyes.

"Hey, gorgeous girls. I'll make doggie dogs for y'all." They kept cheap hot dogs to tempt the puppies with, and both of the girls loved it.

"We might be grilling in the rain." He shrugged. He didn't care, but it made the idea of a shower sort of stupid right now. "You want to get the girls inside?"

"Otherwise, we'll have wet dog smell sunk in the couch again."

"You blame that on the dogs, but really, it was your farts." He laughed, side-stepped Parker's swat and ducked into the house.

"Oh, you little shit." Parker chased him, making grabby hands.

"Nope. Nonono!" He turned the corner into the den, grabbing onto the door jamb for balance.

"Yep. Gonna get you, sweetheart." Parker laughed for him, catching him by the hips.

"You're so fast." He turned in Parker arms, laughing. "Don't hurt me. I have to grill."

"Never going to happen. Never."

He nodded. "I know. You take care of me." He took Parker's left hand and kissed it. He was still so proud of the engagement band on that ring finger, and that Parker had said yes. Every time he saw that ring there, he felt like he had in that moment—happy, in love and grateful.

"Mmm... Love the way your ring looks on my hand."

He blushed, because he probably should be past all of this but he wasn't. "I'm still so amazed and happy you said yes."

"Mmm..." Parker stepped right into his space and lifted his face for a kiss. "We going to shower and then cook or cook and get wet, then shower?"

So many options. "Well, naked things always seem to happen when we shower together."

"Uh-huh... What's your point?" Parker squeezed his ass.

He licked his lips and pressed back into the touch. "Well, are you hungrier for steak, or me?"

"Are you kidding? We can have cereal later."

"Fuck, yeah. Cap'n Crunch, here we come." He caught Parker in a hug and dragged him toward the bathroom. "You stink. You smell like you've been roofing all day."

"Go figure. It's like magic, isn't it?" Parker started pulling off his shirt.

"I wouldn't call it magical, but it's a great excuse for a magical shower." He followed Parker's lead, tugging off his jeans and socks.

"Hot hot or just warm water?" Parker kissed the corner of his mouth.

"Hot hot. Always hot." There wasn't any other way with his fiancé. He let Parker pull him into the shower and everything else disappeared.

"Hey, love." Parker leaned in, his own personal bull rider lifting his face for a kiss.

"Hey, babe. We did good work today." Hell yes, he would take that offer. He bent and kissed Parker, then nipped at his lower lip playfully.

"I like roofing. There's a beginning, a middle, and an end." Parker patted his butt. "Unlike us. We've just got a beginning and then forever."

"Forever sounds about long enough. Maybe. Sex though, that has a beginning, a middle and an end too." He slipped his fingers around Parker's silky balls. "This is the beginning, if you're curious."

"Oh, that's so good to know. Can we have a long, lazy middle?"

"We can. I hear you bull riders love the middle."

"Oh." Parker's eyes lit up. "Very nice. My brilliant lawyer-jack."

"That's me. Brilliant." He understood the assignment. He was going to keep Parker up all night.

And then, if the world worked the way it ought to, tomorrow they'd do it again.

# WANT MORE BA & JODI?

Interested in learning more about our East Meets Westerns?

**Join BA & Jodi's Newsletter**
https://lp.constantcontactpages.com/sl/nzvRTTy

**Patreon:** https://www.patreon.com/BATortuga
There are lots of tiers to chose from, and also free serial stories.
**Discord:** https://discord.gg/Vba5P5Qv
BA's Discord server has a channel for BA/Jodi related chat and info.

*Hey, Y'all!*

We want to thank you for giving A Present for Parker a try. We hope you enjoyed the story and want to check out the rest of the series.

If you can spare a few minutes to post a review at the retail website where you made your purchase, we'd very much appreciate it!

Yeehaw and thanks for reading!

BA & Jodi

# ABOUT JODI

**JODI** takes herself way too seriously and has been known to randomly break out in song. Her queer MCs are imperfect but genuine, stubborn but likable, often kinky, and frequently their own worst enemies. They are characters you can't help but fall in love with while they stumble along the path to their happily ever after. For those looking to get on her good side, Jodi's obsessions include nonfat lattes, basketball (go Celtics!), and tequila any way you pour it.

Website: jodipayne.net

Newsletter: https://readerlinks.com/l/2317334

All Jodi's Social Links: linktr.ee/jodipayne

# ABOUT BA

Western to the bone and an unrepentant Daddy's Girl, BA Tortuga spends her days with her hounds and her beloved wife, having mother-daughter dates, and eating Mexican food. When she's not doing that, she's writing. She spends her days off watching rodeo, knitting, and surfing Pinterest in the name of research. Following their own personal joys, BA and Julia heard the call of the high desert and they now live in the New Mexico mountains. BA's personal saviors include her wife, her best friends, and coffee. Lots of coffee. Really good coffee.

Having written everything from fist-fighting cowboys to rural single dads to werewolves, BA does her damnedest to tell the stories of her heart, which is committed to giving everyone their happily ever after. With books ranging from heart-warming stories of found families, to rodeo cowboys that are fighting to make a mark, to fiery passionate love affairs, BA refuses to be pigeon-holed by anyone but the voices in her head.

BA loves to talk to her readers and can be found at http://batortuga.com/ and her newsletter signup link is <u>http://bit.ly/BAJulianews</u>

# AVAILABLE FROM JODI & BA

## East Meets Westerns

### The On the Ranch Series

Tending Tyler

Roped In

Diamonds in the Rough

Outfoxed

### The Wrecked Universe

Wrecked

Flying Blind

Special Delivery, A Wrecked Holiday Novel

Seeds and Sunshine

Pickup Man

Cowboy for Sale

### The Merry Everything Series

Window Dressing

Cowboy Protection

Cowboys and Cupcakes

Thawed Out

A Present for Parker

### The Higher Elevation Series

Heart of a Cowboy

Keeping Promises

Bigger Than Us

Home Free

## BDSM/Kink

### The Cowboy and the Dom Trilogy

First Rodeo, Book One

Razor's Edge, Book Two

No Ghosts, Book Three

The Soldier and the Angel, a Cowboy and Dom Novel

### The Sin Deep Series

(set in The Cowboy and the Dom Universe)

Sin Deep

Trouble with Cowboys

### The Triskelion Series

Breaking the Rules

Making a Mark

Making the Rules

### Les's Bar Series

Just Dex

Hide Bound

Wholly Trinity

New Tricks

Lost Boy

### The Barn Series

Zeke & Wesley

## Other Titles

**The Collaborations Series**

Refraction

Syncopation

**Puzzles Series**

Cryptic

**Single Titles**

Temptation Ranch

Land of Enchantment

---

**Summit Springs Sapphic (F/F) Romance**

Christmas Bizarre

Honeymoon in the Cards